THOMAS McGUANE'S
TO SKIN A CAT

"Thomas McGuane seems to know all there is to know about upland game, cattle ranches, oil rigs, horses, falconry and the social and economic caste systems of contemporary America. . . . It is our dwindling rural landscapes and their embattled residents that westerner McGuane knows thoroughly, cares for passionately, and describes as sympathetically as any fiction writer at work today."
—CLEVELAND PLAIN DEALER

"Thomas McGuane is a premier American writer, and it is long past time that this fact was made a banner and raised up so that he can read it from horseback in Big Sky country. . . . It is a great gift to have him like Fort Apache set against the glossy lies and sleek trash mouths of our momentarily homogenized state. One celebrates him for calling us 'out East' and for enjoying himself roaming the range, winging one-liners and advancing America's well-armed, California-or-bust cowboy culture into the next century."
—PHILADELPHIA INQUIRER

"The downward spiral from prosperous, snug and well-adapted to despairing and outcast seems nowhere as uncannily seductive as in the fiction of Thomas McGuane."
—THE NEW YORK TIMES BOOK REVIEW

THOMAS McGUANE

TO SKIN A CAT

STORIES

VINTAGE CONTEMPORARIES
VINTAGE BOOKS
A DIVISION OF RANDOM HOUSE
NEW YORK

FOR FRED WOODWORTH

FIRST VINTAGE CONTEMPORARIES EDITION, November 1987

All rights reserved under International and Pan-American Copyright Conventions.
Published in the United States by Random House, Inc., New York, and simultaneously
in Canada by Random House of Canada Limited, Toronto. Originally published, in
hardcover, by Seymour Lawrence, Inc./E.P. Dutton, a division of NAL Penguin Inc.,
in 1986.

Library of Congress Cataloging-in-Publication Data
McGuane, Thomas.
To skin a cat.
(Vintage contemporaries)
I. Title.
[PS3563.A3114T6 1987]   813'.54   87-40093
ISBN 0-394-75521-9 (pbk.)

These stories originally appeared in the following publications: "The Millionaire" in
Ploughshares (Summer 1986); "A Man in Louisiana" in *Shenandoah* (June 1986); "Like
a Leaf" in *Playboy* (January 1983); "Dogs" in *Grand Street* (Spring 1986) and in *Harper's*
(June 1986); "A Skirmish" in *Descant* (Summer 1986); "Two Hours to Kill" in *Mobile
Bay Monthly* (June 1986); "The Rescue" in *Vanity Fair* (September 1986); "Little
Extras" in *Rio Grande* (Spring 1986); "Partners" in *Playboy* (September 1986); "The
Road Atlas" in *Gentleman's Quarterly* (August 1986); "Flight" in *Esquire* (August
1986); and "To Skin a Cat" in *TriQuarterly* (Winter 1981).

Author photo copyright © 1987 by Tom Corcoran

Manufactured in the United States of America

10 9 8 7 6 5 4 3

CONTENTS

THE MILLIONAIRE

It was merely a house beside a lake which had been rented. It was winterized to extend the period of time it could be let, though it was hard to see who would want its view after summer was over. The view was of places just like it, divided by water. It was furnished with the kinds of things owners wish renters to have within the limits of their anxiety about damage, impersonal things. Strangely, the owners stored their golfing trophies here. They were old trophies, and the miniature golfers on them, their bronze coats flaking, belonged to another age. One foot tipped too far; their swings were still British and lacked the freedom of motion American trophy makers later learned to suggest. Something of the reflected stillness of the lake was felt in the living room and the wraparound porch, where the outdoor furniture seemed out of place and the indoor furniture had inadvertently weathered.

Betty was a handsome blonde in her middle forties wearing a green linen Chanel suit. She walked into the house, stooping with two suitcases and managing to clutch the house keys with their large paper tag. Iris, her fifteen-year-old daughter, in the late stages of pregnancy, awkwardly looked for something to do. Betty set the luggage down and stared about with a Mona Lisa smile. She shot a glance at Iris, who was heading for the radio. Iris stopped.

"I guess the landlord saw us coming," said Betty. Iris made an assenting murmur in her throat; it was clear she was yet to develop any real attitude toward this place. "Though blaming him for scenting misfortune seems a bit academic at this stage of the proceedings."

"Mom, where's the thermostat at? I'm getting goose bumps."

"Find it, Iris. It will be on the wall." Iris turned and looked off the porch toward the lake. Betty kept talking. "When we went to stay on the water in my youth—when we went to Horseneck Beach, for example—the water made a nice smell for us. It seemed to welcome us . . . the smell of the ocean. But this lake! Well, it has no odor."

"It's smooth out there. Nice for waterskiing."

"In your condition?" Betty walked to the phone and picked it up. "A dial tone. Good. . . . So, anyway, let's batten down the hatches. You pick yourself a little delivery room. I'm in shock. I have traipsed a hundred miles from my home for a summer surrounded by strangers and their weekend haciendas. If only I'd been clever enough to bring something familiar, my Sanibel shells, anything."

"I'm familiar," said Iris with a pout.

"Not entirely, you're not."

Iris sat down to rest, knowing she shouldn't place her

hands on her stomach complacently. She had come to view its swelling as something strange, and the acceptability of that view comforted her.

The porch and the room had fallen into shadow and the end-table lamps made a yellow glow. Betty stared past her drink while Iris, in her bathrobe, combed out her wet hair. When Jack, who was Betty's husband and Iris's father, came in the house, still dressed for business and somehow out of place in this summer cottage, he first peeked through the partially opened front door with either dread or uncertainty. But when he did come in, he did so as the house's proprietor.

"Hello, Mother."

Betty didn't yield too quickly, so Jack tried Iris.

"How is our royal project?" he asked.

"Hi, Daddy."

Jack clasped his hands before him and turned to Betty. "D'ja stock up? You got Scotch?"

"We have that," said Betty. "We also have some terrifying concoctions belonging to the owner. Mai tai mix. Spañada wine."

"Sid'll be down. Save it for Sid."

Betty asked, "Did you stop off?"

"Nope," said Jack. "This is my first. Cheers."

"Cheers," said Betty. "No, Iris, no record."

"Sid wanted to meet me for one quick one but I said, Do you realize what kind of miles I got in front of me?"

"I think I'll watch sunset from the porch," said Iris without being noticed. She went through the sliding door to the porch, where she felt day fade before the electric lights of the house. If she tried, she could make out what her parents were saying to each other, but she didn't try.

Jack said, "Can she hear us?"

"Who's supposed to bring my stuff up from home?"

"I'm seeing to it. I didn't want to look like we were moving out. The Oakfields were staring from their lawn."

"How come Sid's coming up? Does he have to know?"

"Sid knows all. He's bringing up a low-mileage Caddy Eldo he wants us to try. Burgundy. Vinyl top. The point is, life doesn't have to come to an end. Oh, no."

Betty drifted off. "Could be gorgeous," she said.

"And I predict Judge Anse and his wife will come by. They want to make sure Iris doesn't back out."

"Remind me to thank them for finding us this priceless bide-a-wee. I could smell the wienie roasts from down the beach. This place is like a ball park."

"You can always go home, babe, and return when it's all over."

"Let me get back to you on that."

"I thought Iris was your claim to fame?"

"That's way too simple."

Strangely enough, they toasted this too, touching glasses. Jack winked. Betty said, "You."

That night when they played gin rummy, Betty was the only one who seemed to have any vitality. Jack leaned a tired, stewed face on one hand and stared at the deck with uncaring eyes. Iris played and kept score. Betty played like a demon; she was in a league of her own. She could shuffle like a professional, making an accordion of the cards between her hands.

"My final pregnancy was ectopic," said Betty with an air of peroration. "Otherwise, Iris, you would have had a little baby brother or sister. The ovum—egg to you—the ovum developed in the cervical canal, not in the uterus where the darn thing was supposed to be. Gin!"

"Great," said Jack, "it's over."

"I see the doctor tomorrow," said Iris. "Right?"

Betty gathered all the cards together in a pile. "Iris, I would hope that it's clear why you cannot—repeat, cannot—fritter around in the discard pile and expect to get anywhere."

Betty and Iris worked closely together inserting leaves into the dining room table. As the table expanded, the living room–dining room combination became less of a no-man's-land. Iris and Betty quit shoving and moved around the table, looking at all the comforting empty space on its top. Steaming pots in the kitchenette abetted the festivity.

"Your assignment is to set the table," said Betty. "Are we ten-four on that?"

"Ten-four."

"I will sit at this end, your father at that end. Dr. Dahlstrom goes right there and Miss Whozis, his girlfriend, goes there. If she has a poodle, the poodle remains in the car."

"You don't even know her, Mother."

"I said if there is a poodle. Iris, I love dogs!"

"What about Brucie?"

"Brucie! Brucie was a mongrel, I don't miss him at all. He might have been a dear dog if you weren't designated to pick up after him. No, Brucie would have never been put to sleep if he had learned to potty outside."

"My favorite part of this is the smell of the upstairs cedar closet."

"My favorite part of the whole darn thing was when your father learned of your condition and *burst* into tears. *Boo-hoo-hoo*. Like Red Skelton."

"I meant the house."

Jack seemed to try to come in from work differently every time. That night he ran in the door carrying his briefcase like a hot cannonball. And his voice was elevated.

7

"Dr. Delwyn Dahlstrom and his chiquita are no more than five miles behind me," he cried.

"What of it?" said Betty, smoothing her sleeves. "Our society is reduced to Iris, her gynecologist, and his bimbo. What difference does it make if they're early?"

"I want a shower."

"Not if they're five miles back, kiddo. No way, José."

"Grab me a pick-me-up. I'm gonna go for it."

Jack rose to the occasion. When the doctor came, he pulled open the front door as if revealing the grand prize on a quiz show. Dr. Delwyn Dahlstrom, a portly, grinning Scandinavian, swung his arm to indicate Melanie, a bug-eyed redhead of twenty-five years.

"Melanie," he said, doing the honors.

"We stopped off," Melanie explained, "See, so if we're late, that's how come."

"Who's late?" Betty asked. Only Jack and Iris took it as a crack. Jack spread his arms for the coats. When he got them, he transferred them to Iris and then hurried around the center island to the bartender's side and began pulling noisy levers on ice trays while the others tried to talk.

Jack said, "I remember Delwyn making bathtub gin in the urinalysis machine. Does that date me?"

"You wouldn't happen to have mai tai mix?" Melanie inquired.

"And enough Spañada to sink a battleship," said Betty.

"True," said Dr. Dahlstrom.

"Betty's right," said Melanie. "My taste in drinks is corny."

Dahlstrom's spirits made the dinner a noisy good time for everyone except possibly Iris, who was too young to drink and came to seem almost frozen. And maybe Jack noticed it, even though technically Iris wasn't his department, because he abruptly slumped into his chair and held his head for an odd instant of silence. The others looked at him and it passed.

"Are you feeling baby move regularly?" Dahlstrom asked Iris.

"Yes," said Iris with a red face.

"Has baby changed position in the last month?"

"Not really."

"Any unusual spotting?"

"Ugh!" said Melanie.

"No . . ." said Iris.

"And still our young man has not come forward?" the doctor inquired.

"Delwyn," said Jack, "it goes like this: He has not come forward. Iris is fifteen. Iris is going on with her life. If the young man comes forward, Iris's life doesn't go forward. Use your brain, Delwyn. The story is, Iris goes on with her life."

"And Jack handles the private adoption," Betty added.

Dahlstrom looked all around himself in search of something; then, his focus sharpening, he suddenly noticed Melanie. "Melanie," he said, "go find yourself a snack." This diversionary remark, right after a filling meal, failed to have its intended effect.

"What?" said Melanie. "Betty's going to fill me up on Spañada." Betty pulled a contraption out of the closet, something made of metal tubes and cloth.

"When I get back to the only home I've known since being dragged from Massachusetts as a young bride, it will be Indian summer. Indian summer! To think! I am very lightly complected. So this is going to make a difference on those long days ahead." With a clattering rush of fabric and aluminum, a red and green and yellow beach umbrella sprang open.

Jack said, "Jesus H. Christ." And the doctor said he didn't get it. Melanie said she knew what it was, it was a beach umbrella, and Betty said she still didn't have the dunes of childhood and that that stupid odorless lake out there didn't have so much as a single Pocohontas or other legendary figure associated with it, unless it was the propane man she had been unable to reach on the phone all day.

"In my mind's eye," said Betty, "I will be able to sit next to the Atlantic."

"Bearing Portuguese immigrants," said Jack.

"I will hear—shut up, Jack—the cry of gulls and the moaning of sea buoys."

"I don't get it," said Dr. Dahlstrom. "I thought she was from some burg near Boston."

Jack's sigh seemed to detonate. "Yeah, she is," he said, well within her hearing. "But here's the catch. It had a trolley stop near the water. I'll never hear the end of this if I live to be a hundred."

But Melanie took up for Betty. "I'm like Betty when it comes to mountains. I used to live with my dad in Denver. Even in traffic jams—like going to a Broncos game?—you could see right over the top of the cars all the way to . . . all the way to . . . what was it, Pike's Peak?"

The doctor said, "My favorite is La Jolla."

"I go right on standing for something," said Betty. "Year after year."

"Namely the eternal sea," said Jack. Quite suddenly, he realized that Iris was at the foot of the stairs. She beheld the adults.

"Good night everybody!" she cried. "Thanks for asking!"

It wasn't until she'd gone up and was safely out of earshot that Dr. Dahlstrom said, "Thanks for asking what?"

Everyone but Melanie fell into a kind of state; she stared from one distant gaze to another, then shrugged. Finally, the doctor said, "You got around the courts on the adoption, huh?"

"Yup," said Jack.

"Who's the pigeon?"

"A judge. Yes, a judge, and his hearty but barren wife of thirty years. I like the guy. A real diamond in the rough. State College. Babson-type portfolio of investments. Getting on in years. Wealth. Half hour a day on the rowing machine. Plus, if he morts out, she has family. Betty and I went over this one good."

"How did you find this wonderful fellow?"

The question didn't make Jack comfortable. "Through a thing down at the plant," he said. "We tipped a few. This and that. Said his life had everything but kids. A bulb went off."

Jack looked around to find someone to break the silence. He didn't seem to like this silence at all, and no one was coming forward to break it. Just whose side were they on?

"You know," said Jack, "I'm not the biggest guy on the block. Just a quonset building, a couple of presses. One shift. One time clock. One faithful foreman. I make the calls. I say to the plant, You build it, I'll sell it. I call on everybody. I call on the competition. We make beautiful music together. And then one of my boys, a Polack, sticks his big mitt in a punch press. It goes up next to the roller and never comes out. I offer my most sincere regrets. I don't say, What were you doing with your mitt in the roller? I'm sad for him, but that won't do. No, he wants it all. He wants my business. You can't have it, I say. It's that simple: You can't have it. You can have reasonable compensation, but no more. I want it all, says the Polack. And he has professional counsel who feels so confident, he has taken it on as a contingency bond. I say, You lean on me, I lean on you. I call on the judge, not as a finagler but as a red-blooded American with his own business. I sell myself to the judge. Meanwhile, the Polack's lawyer is sending me poison-pen letters. Shit. You reach a point where you don't know whether you're part of what makes America great or not."

"Eight hours from now," said Dr. Dahlstrom, "I'll be dropping gallstones in a porcelain pan. I can't deal with this."

"You know what I'm in a mood for?" said Melanie. "A diner. Some ham and eggs. The night shift. Neon."

"That is Melanie," said Dahlstrom. "That is her magic."

"I'm going to let those dishes sit till morning," said Betty, apparently overfaced by the magic of Melanie. Conversation trailed off; a car started up; things in the foreground seemed impossible to notice.

Jack wandered over to the bar and made himself a nightcap. He was already in a cloud. Betty went up the stairs and Jack slumped in the peculiar apelike repose produced by patent recliner chairs. But there was a slumberous burn still in his eyes. When Iris came down the stairs in her robe to get some ice cream, Jack smiled at her and kept smiling, finally smiling to himself. The burn went out of his eyes as the sweet sound of the scoop in the ice-cream container reached his ears.

"Daddy," said Iris, "I know this isn't what you wanted to happen." She stopped to think. She was comfortable with Jack. "I realize . . . my condition. But me, so long as it's healthy, at this point I don't care. It did occur. I'm the first to admit that. But aren't we trying to pretend that all this will go away here at the lake? Daddy?"

Jack unfortunately was sound asleep. Among the key effects Betty brought to the lake was Jack's stadium blanket in blue and maize, his school colors. Iris covered him with it, knowing he had to work tomorrow and needed his rest. With the ice cream in one hand, she reached the stairs and turned out the light.

□ □ □

Passing time was a kind of sedative for Betty and Iris. They became like old friends, the kind who can't leave each other on deathbeds. When Jack came home at night he thought they were babbling, and sometimes there was a genuine issue: Iris still wanted the baby; then Betty wanted the baby because of the one she had lost through her ectopic pregnancy; then Betty and Iris thought they could team up and raise the baby. Under the last plan, Jack would have to move out. Even Jack thought so.

They lay out on the lawn with bright tanning reflectors under their chins; they were stretched on lawn chairs; and the heat, the big midwestern heat, was everywhere.

"I realize this is crazy," said Betty. "Sunbathing will make an old bag out of you in a New York minute."

"Did you ever get the name of this lake?" Iris asked.

"Don't move your head when you talk, Iris! You're blinding me!"

"All right."

"I don't know, Lake Polliwog or some fool thing. Don't you wonder what's going on at home? I see grass growing knee high. I see four feet of morning papers on the porch; a storm door slams back and forth in the wind. Maybe the fire department broke in looking for bodies and stole my silver. The TV we left on to discourage burglars has become some kind of haunted Magnavox. It's awful what your mind will do to you. We never got around to putting a decal on the picture window, so the birds with broken necks have gone on piling up. Life just rushes at you and the birds keep dying."

"My feet are swollen."

"This happens."

"And my fingers too."

"Mm-hm," said Betty.

Iris held her hands up in the glare and examined their watery thickness. "I could go for a foreign film right now," she said. "In the picture this girl is pregnant. Out of wedlock in Italy. It's a spa, and Marcello Mastroianni is careless about cigarettes and their effect on the unborn. The spa carries extremely complicated pastries which resemble pretzels. There's a bilingual midwife, and all the cars are low-slung. Sometimes the girl rides in the cars with Mastroianni. Sometimes they pass the evenings playing chess, which they call 'shess.' The girl only knows how to play checkers, which they call 'sheckers.' When she says 'king me,' they are pleasant about it and give the girl soda water, a ring, a buncha stuff. Finally the baby is born, so pink, so perfect and all. They call a wet nurse from the village but the baby won't have a thing to do with this stranger. The baby returns to the girl . . . by suction."

"Iris, that's impossible. A baby can't fly through the air by suction."

"Mom, it's a movie."

"What about Marcello Mastroianni? Does he get around by suction too? When your father was courting me, it was like a real movie. He lived in a boardinghouse. The lady who ran the place raised enormous Belgian hares. And when the lady slept, the Belgian hares guarded the stairs. They had two big teeth in front, and if you didn't go up the stairs in a slow and dignified fashion, one of those huge rabbits would have you by the leg like that!"

"What were you doing up the stairs of Dad's boardinghouse?"

"Not what you think, young lady."

"I'm sure."

Silence; then Betty said, "I'm not going to let this pass."

"So don't."

"I'm terribly afraid that you have confused my morals with your own."

"What a lovely remark," said Iris in a broken voice.

"The truth shall set ye free."

"You bitch."

The two were now sitting up, reflectored heads facing each other like two nodding, miserable sunflowers.

"You won't hear this child calling you what you called me," said Betty. "You won't hear it call you anything."

Betty had always enjoyed her cocktails, but she never drank in the daytime. That changed. It didn't make her sentimental or angry or any of the usual things. It just sped her up. She didn't drink that much, but it was enough to get her darting around and creating an atomosphere of emergency.

One unseasonably cold afternoon, Iris sat dog-earing a paperback with the glass porch doors closed and the oven door open to supplement the baseboard electric heating. Betty was coasting past the windows about the time Jack was expected. Suddenly, she froze in place.

"Here comes your father followed by Sid Katzendorf in a Cadillac! It's the low-mileage Eldo!"

When Jack came in, he was equally excited. Even Iris felt the desperation in this; there had never before been any conversation about Cadillacs. It was just desperate.

"A beauty," Jack said, "and it's loaded. But let's don't rush. You drive it. Try it in a few spots, the freeway, here in the neighborhood. At first it seems like the Queen Mary, but you'll get the hang of it. If you like it, tell Sid to mark it sold. We can swallow the tab. I'll spare you the details. Try the factory air."

When Betty went out the door, things calmed down. Jack had bought Iris a Swiss Army knife, the one that must weigh a pound, and she immediately treasured it. Then they had some orange juice. It almost seemed as if the Cadillac were a decoy. Iris thought Jack loved her.

"Iris," he said, "you're going to survive all this. You're going to finish school. You're going to go to college. If that Polack and his squashed hand don't take my company away from me, I'll give it all to you. How's that sound?"

"It sounds wonderful."

Jack hugged Iris and said, "Then I'll never lose you."

The whole house seemed to go quiet. Iris marked her place and put the book aside. She opened and closed each blade and implement of the knife. He loves me very much, she thought. The evening sun got under the clouds and began to suggest a normal summer evening. The door burst open and Betty ran in, struggling for composure. When she spoke, her voice was tragic and bore the keening finality of a summing up. She quit talking like Massachusetts.

"We're going along the freeway. I see this other Cadillac but it's a two-tone. I'm sitting there trying to think which I like better. Obviously, the driver of the other Caddy is having the exact same thought. We get real close and head for the identical off-ramp. Suddenly it looks like we'll collide. I swerve. I crash into a jalopy. The jalopy takes off."

"That's it?" said Jack.

"That's it."

"Where's Sid?"

"Sid has gone."

"What did he say?"

"He stared at me and said, 'You own it.' "

"Oh, my God."

"Whatever happened to us, Jack. Whatever happened to our luck?" She keened like her own mother out east.

"Is that a question?"

Iris was free to assume what she had brought upon them.

About halfway through the last month of Iris's pregnancy, the adoptive parents came by to meet her.

Betty did it up as an occasion with fresh flowers on the end tables. Jack checked his watch, shot his cuffs, looked out the window at rapid intervals. Iris had been dressed in high-octane maternity clothes: a conical navy blue dress with a whimsical, polka-dotted, droopy bow tie.

At the very moment of the Anses' arrival, Jack seemed to panic. He was frozen in the hallway babbling in a low voice. "They can't find the door. They're gonna walk into the lake!" He started to call out in a high, tinny voice, projecting crazy merriness, "Back there! Right where you parked! You missed it! You missed . . . the front door!"

"Iris!" said Betty. "Animate yourself!"

They finally came inside and the introductions were achieved as the judge looked carefully at everyone, settling finally on Iris, whom he examined at length until she said, "Don't look at me like I was a horse." But the judge took it well and said this was a happy day in their lives. Judge Anse and his wife, Mona, were a couple in their fifties. Judge Anse seemed unable to leave his judicial air at home and put a considerate pause before each remark, a pause that left one feeling scrutinized. His wife looked very scrutinized. It was easy to think that her desire for a baby was all she had left.

"We had a baby once," said Mrs. Anse without varying the tone of her voice. "We had it such a short time we didn't have time to name it. It appeared in the obituary as Baby Anse, comma, girl."

"Are you familiar with ectopic pregnancy?" asked Betty of no one in particular.

"Is it a problem?" said Judge Anse.

"You can say that again."

"Nothing she's got, I hope," said the judge, jerking his thick head toward Iris.

"No, it's something I had," said Betty.

"Oh."

Judge Anse said he worked hard and there was no estate, no one to leave it all to and we can't live forever. That seemed to anger him and he used off-color language. He asked the present company to excuse his French. Iris sat blankly in the middle of a discussion of what a difficult age it was for raising children. It was hard to tell whether this was a reference to Iris or to the age in which the baby would live. But it must have been the latter because Jack said conclusively that the country had nowhere to go but up.

Mrs. Anse kept a level gaze throughout this directed upon Iris. Iris felt this gaze and was ready for anything. When Mrs. Anse smiled and asked her question, Iris was ready. "What was the young fellow like?" she inquired.

"A real gorilla."

"Have we mentioned Iris's grades?" Betty asked. "Straight A's."

"You know," said Mona Anse in a cracking voice, "the agencies wouldn't talk to us. They told us we were too old."

"That's not exactly true," said the judge patiently.

"It is for a Caucasian baby. Old. That's all we heard. We heard it from the state, from the Lutherans, from the Catholics. Old. People suggested every crazy thing you can imagine: midgets, pinheads, boat people. I may be old but I won't be taken advantage of." The judge rested his hand on the back of his wife's.

"Let 'em whine," said Jack to the empty middle of the room. "They're getting a bargain."

Two days later, Iris found out how they met Judge Anse.

"Your father is being sued by a man at the plant who lost something in a machine," said Betty, blandly.

"Lost something?" said Iris. "What?"

"A limb."

"What's that have to do with me?"

"That's how we got to meet Judge Anse. He's hearing the case."

Iris thought for a moment and said, "You sold the baby." It wasn't an accusation.

The night the contractions began, the whole thing almost fell apart. Iris bolted and was found two hours later hiding in a boathouse clear on the other side of the lake. By the time they got her back to the house, Betty was behind with the buffet. Somehow, everything went back into place, and by the time Judge and Mrs. Anse and Dr. Dahlstrom arrived, Iris was secured upstairs. Supplies were laid out. Dahlstrom had been playing golf, and Jack had to lend him some carpet slippers to keep him from marking up the floor with his cleats.

"What are you hoping for?" asked Dahlstrom.

"We don't care as long as it's got five of everything," said the judge. Dahlstrom made a Dagwood sandwich. Betty went up and down the stairs at frequent intervals. Jack seemed edgy but remarked that the leading indicators were up.

Dr. Dahlstrom was balancing his sandwich on one palm and building with the other, when Betty came down and said, "Delwyn, now."

"Hold your horses."

"I can hold mine but I can't hold hers."

"Betty, do me a favor and wait for the pretty part."

Betty came back downstairs and sat while Dahlstrom ate

his sandwich, holding it between bites in front of his admiring gaze like a ship model. When he finished, he said, "And now the good doctor will work his magic. You people pace and wring your hands, whatever blows your hair back." And he went up the stairs.

There was no way to disguise the waiting. Betty mentioned a Big Band Era retrospective on FM but got no response. Everyone was quiet, but Jack seemed to be smoldering. He slumped down inside his suit coat and stared. After a while, he said, "A good deal was had by all." This was not lost on Mrs. Anse.

"To whom do you think you are speaking?" she asked, simultaneously with a moan from the second floor.

"Simmer down, Mona," said Jack. "Simmer down."

"I don't want this ruined."

"Try the salad. Betty used walnut oil."

"This end is well done," said Betty pointing at the roast. "You can see the rare from where you are."

"You'd think I'd feel young tonight. But I don't. I wonder why?" asked the judge.

"Have you tried Grecian Formula Nine?" asked Jack.

"You're a crumb," said the judge. "You're an insufferable crumb."

"And why not?" Jack flared. "I'm about to become a grandfather. How do you think that makes me feel? And Betty, my childhood sweetheart, this whole God damned thing is going to make a grandmother out of her. You know what this means, Judge? This means we're starting to die. That jackass doctor upstairs is shoving us into history."

"If that's how you feel," the judge said.

"That's how we feel."

So, by the time Dr. Dahlstrom arrived at the top of the stairs to announce a successful birth, Jack and the judge were at a stalemate. Jack's moment of vindication lay in his climbing the stairs alone, without looking back, to view the baby lying in its mother's arms. Whatever was going on around her, Iris was too happy and too far away to notice the arrival of Judge Anse and his wife, or to realize that her baby was a millionaire.

That Winter, Ohio Exploration had its meeting at the Grand Hotel in Point Clear, Alabama. Barry Seitz went along as special assistant to Mike Royce, the tough, relatively young president of Ohio Exploration. Barry knew spot checks could happen any time, and as this was his first job that could go anywhere, he memorized everything. The range of subjects ran from drilling reports in various oil plays in the Southeast to orthodonture opinions concerning Mike Royce's impossibly ugly daughter. It was Royce's thought that the girl's dentist was "getting the teeth straight, all right, but blowing her profile." Barry was to "mentally note" that Mike Royce wanted to get together some three- and four-year-old snapshots of the girl and arrange a conference with the dentist. Barry didn't envy the dentist. The girl had inherited her father's profile and would always be a rich little bulldog.

The winter meeting was going to be shortened and therefore compressed because Mike Royce had just decided that he hated the South. So everyone was on edge and the orthodonture issue seemed quite inflamed the longer Royce contemplated his daughter's mouth. Barry could see the pressure forming in his boss's face as he stared past the crab boats making their way across the dead-slick bay. Barry arranged to have some pictures same-day delivered, and he was with his boss when he thumbed through the snapshots.

"I could shit," said Royce from a darkening face. "These kids around here have straight teeth and their folks can't change a lightbulb."

A number of the things Mike Royce said were irritating to Barry, and when Royce was angry he expressed everything in a blur of exposed teeth that made part of Barry think of self-defense. But Barry saw himself on the cusp of failure or success. At thirty, a backward move could be a menace to his whole life; and while he knew he wouldn't be in Royce's employ forever, he wanted to stay long enough to learn oil lease trading so that he could go out on his own. Once he was free he could do the rest of the things he wanted: have a family, tropical fish, remote-control model airplanes. The future was an unbroken sheen to Barry, requiring only irreversible solvency. One of Barry's girlfriends had called him yellow. She went out with the morning trash. Having your ducks in a row does not equal yellow. Barry was cautious.

On the last day of their stay at the Grand Hotel in Point Clear, Alabama, Mike Royce rang for Barry. Barry went down to his room and found Royce in a spotted bathrobe, his blunt feet hooked on the rungs of his chair, staring at the photographs of his daughter arranged chronologically. The little girl's square head did seem to change imperceptibly from picture to picture, though Barry could not tell the influence of hormones from the influence of orthodontic wire. From left to right, the child seemed to be losing character. In picture one she was clearly a vigorous young carnivore, and by picture seven she looked insipid, headed nowhere. It seemed a lot to blame on the dentist, who, Mike Royce pointed out, would be on the carpet Monday first thing. Barry wanted what Mike Royce wanted. So Barry wanted those teeth right.

Now Royce turned his attention to Barry. He did not ask Barry to sit down but seemed to prefer to regard him from his compressed posture in his bathrobe.

"Billy Hebert," he said. "Remember him?" He was spot-checking a mental note.

"Lake Charles," said Barry.

"That's right, a feature player in that deal down there. Now Billy's main lick, for fun, is to hunt birds." He reached Barry a slip of paper. "That dog is in Mississippi. I want you to get it and take it to Billy in Lake Charles."

"Very well."

"If you remember back, we need to be doing something out of this world for Billy. Anyway, chop-chop."

Barry could see the rows of private piers from Royce's window. A few people had gone out carrying crab traps, towels, radios. They seemed to mock Barry's dog-hauling mission with their prospects. But it was better than hearing about the girl's teeth.

A late fall haze from the paper mills outside Mobile hung on the water. The causeway bore a stream of Florida-bound traffic. Bay shrimpers plied the slick, and play-off games sounded from every window of the resort. He knew cheery types lined up in the lobby for morning papers. It wasn't that Barry had less sense of fun than anyone else. He had once alienated a favorite lady friend by yelling "wee!" during sex.

But when riding mowers hummed with purpose on a December day in the Deep South, it seemed cruel and unusual to have to haul a dog from Mississippi to a crooked oil dealer in Louisiana.

The road to the small town in Mississippi on Royce's note wound up from the coastal plain past small cities and shanty-towns. Barry ate at a drive-in restaurant next to an old cotton gin and drove up through three plantations that lay along the Tombigbee in what had been open country of farms and planta-tions. Arms of standing water appeared and disappeared as he soared over leggy trestles heading north. Barry began to be absorbed by his task. Where am I? he thought. He liked the idea of hauling a dog from Mississippi to Louisiana and didn't feel at all demeaned by it as he had back at the Marriott. He passed a monument where the bighearted Union Army had set General Nathan Bedford Forrest free, and he felt giddily—no matter how many GTOs and pizza trucks he passed—that he was going back into time, toward Champion Hill and Shiloh. It seemed every third house had a fireworks stand selling M80s and bottle rockets, and every fifth building was a Baptist church. Oh, variety! he thought, comparing this to Ohio.

He reached Blue Wood, Mississippi, shortly after noon and stopped at a filling station for directions to the house of Jimmy F. Tippett, the man who had advertised the dog. Hearing his accent, the proprietor of the filling station, a round-faced man in coveralls, asked Barry where he came from.

"Chillicothe, Ohio."

The man looked at Barry's face for a moment and said, "Boy, you three-fo' mile from yo' house!"

He took a dirt road out past a gas field, past a huge abandoned WW II ammunition factory and rail spur. The town of Blue Wood had the air of an Old West town with its slightly elevated false-front buildings. Half the stores were empty, and the sidewalks had a few Negroes as the sole pedestrians. Barry drove slowly past the hardware store, where a solitary white man gripped his counter and stared through the front door waiting for customers. "My God," Barry murmured. He couldn't wait to grab that bird dog and run. The teeth of Mike Royce's daughter were behind him, familiar and secure.

Jimmy F. Tippett's house was on the edge of a thousand-acre sorghum field. It was an old house with a metal roof and a narrow dogtrot breezeway. Because of its location, Barry thought it had a faint seaside atmosphere. But above all it spoke of poorness to Barry, and dirty stinking failure; his first thought was, How in the world did this guy lay hands on any dog Mike Royce would buy? Hunching over in the front seat after he'd parked, Barry gave way to temptation and opened Royce's envelope with a thumbnail. Inside was two thousand dollars in crisp hundreds. This, thought Barry, I've got to see.

He got out of the car, walking around the back of it so he could use it as a kind of blind while he looked things over. There were great big white clouds in the direction past the house and a few untended pecan trees. There had been a picket fence all around, but it looked like cattle or something had just walked it down into the ground. Here and there a loop of it stood up, and the pickets were weathered of most of their white paint and shaped at their ends like clubs in a deck of cards. Barry tried vainly to relate this to his career. In fact, how would Mike Royce and his accountants view this trip? He guessed it would have to be Travel and Entertainment.

The pattern of shadows on the screen door changed and Barry interrupted his thought to recognize that one of the shadows must now be Jimmy F. Tippett. So he strode up to the house, gulping impressions, and said, "Mr. Tippett, is that you?"

"Yes, sir," came a voice.

"I'm Barry Seitz. I represent Mr. L. Michael Royce. I'm here about a dog."

The screen door opened. Inside it stood a small man about sixty years of age, in khaki pants and starched white shirt. He had an auto insurance company pen holder in his pocket and a whistle around his neck. His face was entirely covered by fine dark wrinkles. A cigarette hung from the corner of his mouth. He looked Barry over as though he were doing a credit check. "Tippett," he said. "Come in."

Barry walked in. It appeared that Tippett lived entirely in one room. "I can't stay but a minute. I've got to get this dog to Louisiana."

"Have a seat," said Tippett. Barry moved backward and slipped into a chair. Tippett watched him do it. "I'll get the whiskey out," said Tippett. "Help you unwind."

"I'm quite relaxed," said Barry defiantly, but Tippett got down a bottle from a pie safe that held the glasses too.

"You want water or S'em-Up?" asked Tippett.

"Neat," said Barry.

"You what?"

"Just straight would be fine," Barry said. Tippett served their whiskey and sat down next to his television set. His drink hand moved slightly, a toast. Barry moved his. It was quiet.

"You go to college?" asked Tippett.

"Yes," said Barry, narrowly avoiding the words *Ohio State*. "And you?" he asked. Tippett did not answer, and Barry feared he'd taken it as a contemptuous question. Nevertheless, he decided not to go into anything long about college being a waste of time. In fact, Barry had a sudden burst of love for his old college. He felt a small ache looking around the bare room for days of wit and safety before he'd been out and about on unfathomable missions like this one. Dogs, tooth pictures, oil crooks, a secure future. Tippett was humming a tune and look-ing around the room. I know that tune, thought Barry, It's "Yankee Doodle Dandy." You bastards fired on our flag first. Fort Sumter.

"What's that song you're whistling?"

"Oh, a old song."

"Really! I sort of remember it as a favorite of mine."

"That's nice. Yes, sir, that's nice. Some of these songs nowadays, why, I don't like them. They favor shit to me." There was a worn-out shotgun in the corner, boots, a long rope with a snap on it.

"Let's have a look at this famous dog," said Barry.

"Ain't famous."

"Expensive."

"Expensive? I got about twenty-five cents an ar to wuk the prick."

Tippett whistled through his teeth, and a pointer came in from the next room on his belly and laid his head on Tippett's knee. "There he is, Old Bandit."

"He's good looking," said Barry.

"He get better lookin' when you turn him a-loose. He'll slap find birds. He a gentleman's shooting dog De Ville. Use a section bean field in five minute. Fellow need enough country for a dog like Bandit. Bandit a foot dog, a truck dog, and a horseback dog. Bandit everything they is. He broke to death but he'll run off on a fool, now."

Barry had caught up on the word *gentleman*. A gentle-man's dog. He could see all this, somehow, in the words of the ardent old Tippett. He looked at fidelity writ large in the peaceful bird dog's anciently carved head and was entirely unable to picture the kind of fool he'd run off on. This was a landowner's dog, he sensed, and he mildly resented having to pack him to Louisiana.

"I wish I owned this dog," said Barry.

"I do too," said Tippett, staring once again at L. Michael Royce's money. "This any good?" he asked, holding it up. Barry just nodded. He was entirely in the world of Tippett, feeling the senselessness of trading the money for Bandit. Now the atmosphere was heavy with the idea of lost dog.

A long silence followed. Barry felt that a kind of intimacy had formed. This man had something that he and Royce and the man in Louisiana wanted, but now he had gone over to the other side. When he took the dog to the car on a lead, Tippett said, "I was sixty-six in August. I'll never have another dog like that." When he went to the house, he didn't pet Bandit; he never looked back.

Barry started down the road with Bandit on the seat beside him. As he went back through Blue Wood, the huge clouds he had noticed driving to Tippett's seemed to enlarge with the massive angular light of evening, and the empty buildings of the town looked bombed out and derelict. A man was selling barbecue from an outdoor smoker. Barry stopped and ate some pork and slaw while he looked at the four-way roads trailing off into big fields. He thought, I'd like to give that dog a whirl. The man rolled down the lid on the smoker.

"Like anything to drink?"

"S'em-Up," said Barry. He had decided he would run Bandit.

Barry drove alongside the vast soybean field with its tangle of stalks and curled leaves and long strips of combined ground. There were hedgerows of small hardwoods wound about with osage orange and kudzu. Some of the fields had gas wells, and at one county-road corner there was a stack of casing pipe and a yellow backhoe as battered as an army tank. When the road came to an end, the bean fields stretched along a stream course and over low rounded hills as far to the west as Barry could see. This is it, he thought, and stopped.

Bandit stirred and whined when the engine shut off. He sat up and stared through the windshield at the empty space. It made Barry apprehensive to not quite understand what riveted his attention so. I wish I had more information, he thought, a little something more to go by. Nevertheless, he turned Bandit loose and thought for the short time he saw him that Tippett was right, that he got prettier and prettier, in his burning race over the horizon.

He was gone. It was as though Mike Royce towered up out of the Mississippi horizon to stare down at Barry in his rental car, clutching the orthodonture photographs and Barry's employment contract.

He got out and started running across the bean field. He ran so fast and uncaringly that the ground seemed to rise and fall beneath him as he crossed the hills. He hit a piece of soft plowed ground and it sapped his strength so quickly he found himself stopped, his hands gripping his knees. Oh, Bandit, he cried out, come back!

Just before dusk, he came through a grove of oak on the edge of a swamp. A cold mist had started up in fingers toward the trees, and at their very edge stood Bandit on point, head high, sipping the breeze, tail straight as a poker, in a trance of found birds. Barry thought he cried out to Bandit but he wasn't sure, and he knew he didn't want to frighten him into motion. He walked steadily in Bandit's direction. The dog stood at his work, not acknowledging him. When he was about a hundred feet away, the covey started to flush. He froze as birds roared up like brown bees and swarmed into the swamp. But Bandit stood still and Barry knew he had him. He admired Tippett's training in keeping Bandit so staunch and walked to the dog in an agony of relief. Good Bandit, he said, and patted his head, Bandit's signal to go on hunting: He shot into the swamp.

The brambles along the watery edge practically tore his clothes off. His hands felt sticky from bloody scratches. By turns he saw himself strangling Royce, Tippett, and the man in Louisiana. He wondered if Royce would ever see him as a can-do guy again. From Cub Scouts on he had had this burden of reliability, and as he felt the invisible dog tearing it away he began to wonder why he was running so fast.

He reached higher ground and a grove of hickories with a Confederate cemetery, forty or fifty unknown soldiers. He sat down to rest among the small stones, gasping for air. What he first took to be the sound of chimes emerging distantly from the ground turned out to be his own ringing ears. It occurred to him that some of the doomed soldiers around him had gone to their deaths with less hysteria and terror than he had brought to the chase for this dog. Maybe it wasn't just the dog, he thought, and grew calm. Maybe it was that little bitch and her crooked teeth.

It was dark and Barry gave himself up to it. A symphonic array of odors came up from the ground with the cooling night, and he imagined the Confederate bones turning into hickory trees over the centuries. Shade, shelter from the wind, wood for ax handles, charcoal for barbecue. S'em-Up. Bones.

But, he thought, standing, that dog isn't dead yet; and he resumed his walk. He regained open country somehow and walked in a gradual curve that he thought would return him to his car. He thought his feet remembered the hills but he wasn't sure and he didn't care. His eyes recorded the increasing density of night until he could no longer see the ground under him. The moon rose and lit the far contours of things, but close up the world was in eclipse. In a while, he came to the edge of a pond. Only its surface could be seen like a sheet of silver hanging in midair. As he studied it, trying to figure out how to go around, the shapes of horses materialized on its surface. He knew they must be walking on the bank, but the bank itself was invisible and the only knowledge of horses he had was the progress of their reflection in the still water. When the horses passed, he walked toward the water until he saw his own shape. He watched it disappear and knew he'd gone on around.

Back in the bean field, Barry felt a mild wave of hysteria pass over him once more, one in which he imagined writing a memo to Royce about having been knee-deep in soybean futures, much to report, et cetera, et cetera; by the way, couldn't seem to lay hands on Louisiana man's dog, et cetera, et cetera. Hope dog-face girl's teeth didn't all fall out. More later, yrs, B. After which, he felt glumly merry and irresponsible.

When he got to his car, it occurred to him that this had all happened a couple of miles from Tippett's house. No great distance for a hyena like Bandit. So he drove over there, to find the house unlighted and silent. He walked to the door. A bark broke out and was muffled. Barry knocked. The door opened and Tippett said, "I thought you went to Louisiana."

"Hand him over," said Barry.

"Come in," said Tippett. Barry walked into the empty room. Tippett had a loose T-shirt on, and his pants were held by the top button only. Barry looked all around and saw nothing. He felt uncertain.

"Didn't Bandit come back?"

Tippett didn't answer. He just sat down and poured from the whiskey bottle that was right where he'd left it earlier. "You lose that dog?" he asked. Something tapped across the floor in the next room. *He doesn't want to go to Louisiana,* he thought, *and he surely doesn't want to go with me.* A wave of peace came over him.

"Yeah, I did," said Barry, rising in his own esteem. The

old man studied him closely, studied his face and every little thing he did with his hands. Barry raised his glass to his lips, thinking only of the movement and the whiskey. He quit surveying the old man's possessions and wondering what time it was somewhere else.

"What do you suppose would make a trained dog just go off and leave like that?" Barry asked.

The old man made a sound in his throat, almost clearing it to speak something which must not be misunderstood. "Son," he said, "anything that'll eat shit and fuck its own mother is liable to do anything." The two men laughed as equals.

Barry thought of the men down in the Confederate grave-yard. He considered the teeth of Mike Royce's daughter and his own "future." Above all, he thought of how a dog could run so far that, like too many things, it never came back.

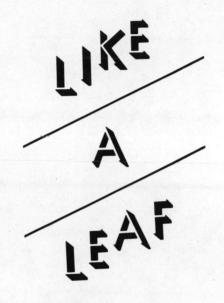

I'm underneath my small house in Deadrock. The real estate people call it a "starter" home, however late in life you buy one. It's a modest house that gives you the feeling that either you're going places or that this won't do. This starter home is different; this one is it.

From under here, I can hear the neighbors talking. He is a successful man named Deke Patwell. His wife is away and he is having an affair with the lady across the street, a sweet and exciting lady I've not met yet. Frequently he says to her, "I am going to impact on you, baby." Today, they are at one of their many turning points.

"I think I'm coming unglued," she says.

"Now, now."

"I don't follow," she says with a little heat.

"All is not easy."

"I got that part, but when do we go someplace nice?" She has a beautiful voice, and underneath the house I remember she is pretty. What am I doing here? I'm distributing bottle caps of arsenic for the rats that come up from the river and dispute the cats over trifles. I represent civilization in a small but real way.

Deke Patwell laughs with wild relief. Once I saw him at the municipal pool, watching young girls. He was wearing trunks and allergy-warning dog tags. What a guy! To me he was like a crude foreigner or a gaucho.

Anyway, I came down here because of the rats. Read your history: they carry Black Plague. Mrs. Patwell was on a Vegas excursion with the Deadrock Symphony Club.

When I get back inside, the flies are causing a broad dumb movement on the windows. We never had flies like this on the ranch. We had songbirds, apple blossoms, and no flies. My wife was alive then and saw to that. We didn't impact, we loved each other. She had an aneurism let go while carding wool. She just nodded her pretty face and headed out. I sat there like a stupe. They came for her and I just knocked around the place trying to get it. I headed for town and started seeing the doctor. Things came together: I was able to locate a place to live in, catch the Series, and set up housekeeping. Plus, the Gulch, everyone agrees, is Deadrock's nicest neighborhood. A traffic violator is taken right aside and lined out quick. It's a neighborhood where folks teach the dog to bring the paper to the porch, so a guy can sit back in his rocker and find out who's making hamburger of the world. I was one of this area's better cattlemen, and town life doesn't come easy. Where I once had coyotes and bears, I now have rats. Where I once had the oldtime marriages of my neighbors, I now have Impact Man poking a real sweet gal who never gets taken someplace nice.

My eating became hit-or-miss. All I cared about was the
World Series after a broken season. I was high and dry, and
when you're like that you need someone or something to take
you away. Death makes you different like the colored are
different. I felt I was under the spell of what had happened to
me. Then someone threw a bottle onto the field in the third or
fourth game of the Series and almost hit the Yankee left fielder,
Dave Winfield. I felt completely poisoned. I felt like a rat with
a mouthful of bottle caps. All my sense of fairness was settled
on Winfield, who is colored, like I felt having been in the
company of death. Then Winfield couldn't hit the ball anyway,
and just when Reggie Jackson got his hitting back, what happens? He drops an easy pop fly.

What were my wife and I discussing when she died? The
Kona Coast. It seems so small. Sometimes when I think how
small our topic was, I feel the weight of my hair tearing at my
face. I bought a youth bed to reduce the size of the unoccupied
area. The doctor says because of the shaking, I get quite a little
bit less rest per hour than the normal guy. Rapid eye movement,
and so on.

Truthfully speaking, part of me has always wanted to live in
town. You hear the big milling at the switching yard and, on
stormy nights, the transcontinental trucks reroute off the inter-
state, and it's busy and kind of like a last-minute party at
somebody's house. The big outfits are parked all over with their
engines running, and the heat shivers at the end of the stacks.
The old people seem brave trying to get around on the ice: one
fall and they're through, but they keep chunking, going on
forward with a whole heck of a lot of grit. That fact gives me
a boost.

And I love to window-shop. I go from window to window alongside people I don't know. There's never anything I

want in there, but I feel good because I am excited when somebody picks out a daffy pair of shoes or a hat you wouldn't put on your dog. My wife couldn't understand this. Nature was a shrine to her. I wanted to see people more than she did. Sit around with just anybody and make smart remarks. Sometimes I'd pack the two of us into the hills. My wife would be in heaven. I'd want to buy a disguise and slip off to town and stare through the windows. That's the thing about heaven. It comes in all sizes and shapes.

Anyone in my position feels left behind. It's normal. But you got to keep picking them up and throwing them; you have got to play the combinations or quit. What I'd like is a person, a person I could enjoy until she's blue in the face. This, I believe. When the time comes, stand back from your television set.

I don't know why Doc keeps an office in the kind of place he does, which is merely the downstairs of a not-so-good house. I go to him because he is never busy. He claims this saves him the cost of a receptionist.

Doc and I agree on one thing: it's all in your head. The only exception would be aspirin. Because we believe it's all in your head, we believe in immortality. Immortality is important to me because, without it, I don't get to see my wife again. Or, on the lighter side, my dogs and horses. That's all you need to know about the hereafter. The rest is for the professors, the regular egghead types who don't have to make the payroll. We agree about my fling with the person. I hope to use Doc's stethoscope to hear the speeding of the person's heart. All this has a sporting side, like hunting coyotes. When Doc and I grow old and the end is in sight, we're going to become addicted to opium. If we get our timing wrong, we'll cure ourselves with aspirin. We plan to see all the shiny cities, then adios. We speak of cavalry firefights, Indian medicine, baseball, and pussy.

Doc doesn't come out from behind the desk. He squints, knowing I could lie, then listens.

"My house in town is going to work fine. The attic has a swing-down ladder and you look from a round window up there into the backyards. You can hear the radios and see people. Sometimes couples have little shoving matches over odd things, starting the charcoal or the way the dog's been acting. I wrote some of them down in a railroad seniority book to tell you. They seem to dry up quick."

"Still window-shopping?"

"You bet."

"If you don't buy something soon, you're going to have to give that up."

"I'll think about it," I say.

"What have you been doing?"

"Not a whole heck of a lot."

"See a movie, any movie."

"I'll try."

"Take a trip."

"I can't."

"Then pack for one and don't go."

"I can do that."

"Stay out of the wind. It makes people nervous, and this is a windy town. Do what you have to do. You can always find a phone booth, but get out of that wind when it picks up. And any time you feel like falling silent, do it. Above all, don't brood about women."

"Okay. Anything else?"

"Trust aspirin."

"I've been working on my mingling."

"Work on it some more."

"Doc," I say, "I've got a funny feeling about where I'm headed."

"You know anybody who doesn't?"

"So what do I do?"

"Look at the sunny side. Anyway, I better let you go. There's someone in the lobby with Blue Cross."

So I go.

By hauling an end table out to the porch, despite that the weather is not quite up to it, and putting a chair behind it, I make a fine place for my microwave Alfredo fettucini. I can also watch our world with curiosity and terror. If necessary, I can speak when spoken to, by sipping my icewater to keep the chalk from my mouth.

A car pulls up in front of Patwells'; Mrs. Patwell gets out with a small Samsonite and goes to the house. That saves me from calling a lot of travel agents. The world belongs to me.

I begin to eat the Alfredo fettucini, slow, spacing each mouthful. After eating about four inches of it, I see the lady from across the street, the person, on the irregular sidewalk, gently patting each bursting tree trunk as she comes. Since I am now practically a mute, I watch for visible things I can predict. And all I look for is her quick glance at Deke Patwell's house and then a turn through her chain-link gate. I love that she is pretty and carries nothing, like the Chinese ladies Doc tells me about who achieve great beauty by teetering around on feet that have been bound. I feel I am listening to the sound of a big cornfield in springtime. My heart is an urgent thud.

To my astonishment, she swings up her walk without a look. Her wantonness overpowers me. Impossible! Does she not know the wife is home from Vegas?

I look up and down the street before lobbing the Alfredo fettucini to a mutt. He eats in jerking movements and stares at me like I'm going to take it back. Which I'm quite capable of doing, but won't. I have a taste in my mouth like the one you get in those frantic close-ins hunting coyotes. I feel like a happy crook. Sometimes when I told my wife I felt this way, she was touched. She said I had absolutely no secret life. The sad thing is, I probably don't.

I begin sleeping in the attic. I am alone and not at full strength, so this way I feel safer. I don't have to answer door or phone. I can see around the neighborhood better, and I have the basic timing of everybody's day down pat. For example, the lady goes to work on time but comes home at a different hour every day. Does this suggest that she is a carefree person to whom time means nothing or who is, perhaps, opposed to time's effects and therefore defiant about regularity? I don't know.

Before I realize it, I am window-shopping again. Each day there is more in the air, more excitement among the shoppers, who seem to spill off the windows into the doors of the stores. The sun is out and I stand before the things my wife would never buy, not risqué things but things that wouldn't stand up. She seems very far away now. But when people come to my store windows, I sense a warmth that is like friendship. Any time I feel uncomfortable in front of a particular store, I move to sporting goods, where it is clear that I am okay, and besides, Doc is fixing me. My docile staring comes from the last word in tedium: guns and ammo, compound bows, fishing rods.

When I say that I am okay, I mean that I am happy in the company of most people. What is wrong with me comes from my wife having unexpectedly died and from my having read the works of Ralph Waldo Emerson when my doctor and I were boning up on immortality. But I am watching the street, and something will turn up. In the concise movements of the person I'm most interested in, and in the irregularity of her returns, which she certainly despises, I sense a glow directed toward me, the kind of light in a desolate place that guides the weary traveler to his rest.

Today, she walks home. She is very nearly on time. She walks so fast her pumps clatter on our broken Deadrock sidewalk. She swings her shoulder bag like a cheerful weapon and arcs into the street automatically to avoid carelessly placed sprinklers. She touches a safety match to a long filter brand, as she surveys her little yard, and goes in. She works, I understand, at the County Assessor's office, and I certainly imagine she does a fine job for those folks. With her bounce, her cigarettes, and her iffy hours, she makes just the kind of woman my wife had no use for. Hey! It takes all kinds. Human life is thus filled with variety, and if I have a regret in my own so far, it is that I have not been close to that variety: that is, right up against it.

I need a break and go for a daylight drive. I take the river road through the foothills north of Deadrock—a peerless jaunt—to our prison. It is an elegant old dungeon that has housed many famous Western outlaws in its day. The ground it rests on was never farmed, having gone from buffalo pasture to lockup many years ago. Now it has razor wire surrounding it and a real up-to-date tower like out east.

One man stands in blue light behind its high windows. When you see him from the county road, you think, That certainly must be the loneliest man in the world. But actually, it's not true. His name is Al Costello and he's a good friend of mine. He's the head of a large Catholic household, and the tower is all the peace he gets. The lonely guy is the warden, an out-of-stater, a professional imprisoned by card files: a man no one likes. He looks like Rock Hudson, and he can't get a date.

Sometimes I stop in to see Al. I go up into the tower and we look down into the yard at the goons and make specific comments about the human situation. Sometimes we knock back a beer or two. Sometimes I take a shot at one of his favorite ball clubs, and sometimes he lights into mine. It's just human fellowship in kind of a funny spot.

But, today I keep on cruising, out among the jackrabbits and sagebrush, high above the running irrigation, all the way around the little burg, then back into town. I stop in front of the doughnut shop, waiting for the sun to travel the street and open the shop, and herald its blazing magic up commercially zoned Deadrock. Waiting in front is a sick-looking young man muttering to himself at a high relentless pitch of the kind we associate with Moslem fundamentalism. At eight sharp the door opens, and the Moslem and I shoot in for the counter. He seems to have lost something by coming inside, and I am riveted upon his loss. By absolute happenstance, we both order glazed. Then I add an order of jelly-filled which I deliver, still hot, to the lady's doorstep.

I'm going to stop reading this newspaper. In one week, the following has been reported: A Deadrock man shot himself fatally in a bar, demonstrating the safety of his pistol. Another man, listening to the rail, had his head run over by every car of a train that took half an hour to go by. Incidents like these make it hard for me to clearly see the spirit winging its way to heaven. And though I would like to stop reading the paper, I really know I won't. It would set a bad example for the people on the porches who have trained Spot to fetch.

"Did you get the doughnuts?" I called out that evening.

Tonight, as I fall asleep, I have a strange thought indeed.

It goes like this: Darling (my late wife), I don't know if you are watching all this or not. If you are, I have but one request: Put yourself in my shoes. That's quite an assignment, but give it the old college try for the sake of yours truly.

I know they've been talking when I see Deke Patwell give me the fishy look. I cannot imagine which exact locution she used —probably that I was "bothering" her—but she has very evidently made of me a fly in Deke's soup. There is not a lot he could do, standing next to his warming-up sensible compact, but give me this look and hope that I will invest it with meaning. I decide to blow things out of proportion.

"You two should do something *nice* together!" I call out.

Deke slings his head down and bitterly studies a nail on one hand, then gets in and drives away.

You think you got it bad? Says here a man over to Arlee was jump-starting his car in the garage; he had left it in gear, and when he touched the terminals of the battery the car shot forward and pinned him to a compressor that was running. This man was inflated to four times his normal size and was still alive after God knows how long when they found him. A hopeful Samaritan backed the car away and the man just blew up on the garage floor and died. As awful as that is, it adds nothing whatsoever to the basic idea. Passing in your sleep or passing as a pain-crazed human balloon on a greasy garage floor produces the same simple result year after year. The major differences lie among those who are left behind. If you're listening, please understand I'm still trying to see why we don't all cross the line on our own, or why nice people don't just help us on over. Who knows if you're even listening?

□ □ □

"So," I cry out to the person with exaggerated innocence, illustrating how I am crazy like a fox. "So, how did you enjoy the doughnuts?"

She stops, looks, thinks. "That was you?"

"That was me."

"Why?" She is walking toward me.

"It was a little something from someone who thinks somebody should take you somewhere nice."

My foot is in the door. It feels as big as a steamboat.

"Tomorrow," she says from her beautiful face, "make it cinnamon Danish." Her eyes dance with cruel merriment. I feel she is of German extraction. She has no trace of an accent, and her attire is domestic in origin. I think, What am I saying? I'm scaring myself. This is a Deadrock local with zip for morals.

I decided to leap forward in the development of things to ascertain the point at which it doesn't make sense. We are very much in love, I say to myself. I recoil privately at this thought, knowing I am still okay if not precisely tops. I am neither a detective nor a complete stupe. Like most of the human race, I fall somewhere in between.

"Tell you what," she says with a twinkle. "I come home from work and I freshen up. Then you and me go for a stroll. How far'd you get?"

"Stroll . . . "

"You're a good boy tonight and I let you off lightly."

Mercy. My neck prickles. She laughs in my face and heads out. I see her cross the trees at the end of the street. I see the changing flicker of different-colored cars. I see mountains beyond the city. I see her bouncing black hair even after she has gone. I say quietly, I'm lonely; I had no idea you were not to have a long life. But I'm still in love.

I call Doc. I tell him, You can put your twenty-two fifty

an hour where the sun don't shine, you dang quack. John Q. Public says, walk the line, boy, or pay the price. Well, John, the buck stops here. I'm going it alone.

She stood me up and it's midnight.

I have never felt like this. This house doesn't belong to me. It belongs to the person, and I'm lying on her bed viewing the furnishings. It's dark here. I can see her coming up the sidewalk. She will come alongside the house and come in through the kitchen. I am in the back room. I guess I'll say hello.

"Hello."

"Hello." She's quite the opposite of my wife, but it's fatal if she thinks this is healthy. She's in the same blue dress and appears to view this as a clever seduction. "It's you. Who'd have guessed? I'm going to bathe, and if you ask nice you can help."

"I want to see."

"I know that." She laughs and goes through the door undressing. "Just come in. You'll never get your speech right. Do I look drunk? I am a little. I suppose your plan was a neighborhood rape." Loud laugh. She hangs the last of her clothes and studies me. Then she leans against the cupboards. "Please turn the water on, kind of hot." When I turn away from the faucets she is sitting on the side of the tub. I think I am going to fall but I go to her and rock her in my arms so that she kind of spreads out against the white porcelain.

She looks at me and says, "The nicest thing about you is you're frightened. You're like a boy. I'm going to frighten you as much as you can stand." I undress and we get into the clear water. I look at the half of myself that is underwater; it looks like something at Sea World. Suddenly, I stand up.

"I guess I'm not doing so good. I'm not much of a rapist after all." I get out of the tub, a tremendous stupe.

"You're making me feel great."

"That Deke has caused you to suffer."

"Oh, crap."

"It's time he took you someplace nice." I'm on the muscle now.

I am drying off about a hundred miles an hour. I go into the next room and pull on my trousers. I don't even see her coming. She pushes me over on the daybed and drags my pants back off. I am so paralyzed all I can do is say, Please no, Please no, as she clambers roughly atop me and takes me, almost hurting me with her fury, ending with a sudden dead flop. Every moment or so, she looks at me with her raging victorious eyes.

"Just don't turn me in," she says. "It would be awful for your family." She bounces up and returns to the bathroom while I dress again. There is a razor running and periodic splashes of water. Whether it is because my wife has to sit through the whole thing or that I can't bring her back, I don't know, but the whole thing makes me a different guy. In short, I've been raped.

She tows me outside, clattering on the steps in wooden clogs, sending forth a bright woman's cologne to savage my nerves. I see there is only one way my confused hands can regain their grasp: I burst into tears. She pops open a small flowered umbrella and uses it to conceal me from the outside world. It seems very cozy in there. She coos appropriately.

"Are you going to be okay now?" she asks. "Are you?" I see Deke's car coming up the street. The Impact Man, the one who never does anything nice for her. I dry my tears posthaste. We head down the street. We are walking together in the bright evening sky under our umbrella. This foolishness implies an intimacy that must have gone hard with Impact Man, because he arcs into his driveway and has to brake hard to keep from going through his own garage with its barbecue, hammocks, and gap-seamed neglected canoe, things whose hopes of a future seem presently to ride on the tall shapely legs of my companion.

I can't think of something really right for us. The only decent restaurant would seem as though we were on a date, put us face to face. We need to keep moving. I feel pretty certain we could pop up and see Al Costello, my Catholic friend in the tower. He always has the coffeepot going. So we get into my flivver and head for the prison. It makes a nice drive in a Tahiti-type sunset, and by the time I graze Staff Parking to the vast space of Visitors, the wonderful blue-white of the glass tower has ignited like the pilot light on a gas stove.

"I want you to meet a friend of mine," I tell the lady. "Works here. Big Catholic family. He's a grandfather in his late thirties. It looks like a lonely job and it's not."

The tower has an elevator. The gate guards know me and we sail in. The door opens in the tower.

"Hey," I say.

"What's cooking?" Al grins vacantly.

"Thought we'd pop up. Say, this is a friend of mine."

"Mighty pleased," Al says. He has the lovely manners of someone battered beyond recognition. She now glues herself to the window and stares at the cons. I think she has made some friendly movements to the guys down in the yard. I glance at Al and evidently he thinks so too. We avert our glances and Al says, "Can I make a spot of coffee?" I feel like a fool.

"I'm fine," she says. "Fine." She is darn well glued to the glass. "Can a person get down there?"

"Oh, a person could," says Al. I notice he is always in slow movement around the tower, always looking, in case some geek goes haywire. "Important thing I guess is that no one can come here unless I let them in. They screen this job. The bad apples are soon gone. It takes a family man."

"Are those desperate characters?" She asks, gazing around. I move into the window and look down at the minnowlike movement of the prisoners. This would have held zero interest for my wife.

"A few, I guess. This is your regular backyard prison. No celebrities. We've got the screwballs is about all we've got."

"How's the family, Al." I dart in.

"Fine, just fine."

Everybody healthy?"

"Oh, yeah. Andrea Elizabeth had strep but it didn't pass to nobody in the house. Antibiotics knocked it for a loop."

"And the missus?"

"Same as ever."

"For Christ's sake," says my companion. We turn. He and I think it's us. But it's something in the yard. "Two fairies," she says through her teeth. "Can you beat that?"

After which she just stares out the windows while Al and I drink some pretty bouncy coffee with a nondairy creamer that makes shapes in it without ever really mixing. It is more or less to be polite that I drink it at all. I look over, and she has her wide-spread hands up against the glass like a tree frog. She is grinning very hard and I know she has made eye contact with someone down in the exercise yard. Suddenly, she turns.

"I want to get out of here."

"Okay," I say brightly.

"You go downstairs," she says. "I need to talk to Al."

"Okay, okay."

My heart is coated with ice. Plus, I'm mortified. But I go downstairs and wait in a green-carpeted room at the bottom of the stairs. There is a door out and a door to the yard. I think I'll wait here. I don't want to sit in the car trying to look like I'm not abetting a jail break. I'm going downhill fast.

I must be there twenty minutes when I hear the electronics

of the elevator coming at me. The stainless doors open and a very disheveled Al appears with my friend. There is nothing funny or bawdy in her demeanor. Al swings by me without catching a glance and begins to open the door to the yard with a key. He has a service revolver in one hand as he does so. "Be cool now, Al," says my friend intimately. "Or I talk."

The steel door winks and she is gone into the prison yard. "We better go back," says Al in a doomed voice. "I'm on duty, God almighty."

"Did I do this?" I say in the elevator.

"You better stay with me. I can't have you leaving alone." He unplugs the coffee mechanically. When I get to the bullet-proof glass, I can see the prisoners migrating. There is a little of everything: old guys, stumblebums, Indians, Italians, Irishmen, all heading into the shadow of the tower. "We're just going to have to go with this one. There's no other way." He looks crummy and depleted but he is going to draw the line. We have to go with it. She will signal the tower, he tells me. So we wait by the glass like a pair of sea captain's wives in their widow's walks. It goes on so long, we forget why we're waiting. We are just doing our job.

Then there is a small reverse migration of prisoners and she, bobby pins in her teeth, checking her hair for bounce, waves up to us in the tower. We wave back in this syncopated motion which is almost the main thing I remember, me and Al flapping away like a couple of widows.

As we ride down in the elevator again, Al says, "You take over from here." And we commence to laugh. We laugh so hard I think one of us will upchuck. Then we have to stop to get out of the elevator. We cover our mouths and laugh through our noses, tears streaming down our cheeks, while Al tries to get the door open. Our lady friend comes in real sternlike, though, and we stop. It is as if we'd been caught at something and she is awful sore. She heads out the door and Al gives me the gun.

In the car, she says with real contempt, "I guess it's your turn." Buddy, was that the wrong thing to say.

"I guess it is." I am the quiet one now.

There is a great pool on the river about a mile below the railroad bridge. It's moving but not enough to erase the stars from its surface, or the trout sailing like birds over its deep pebbly bottom. The little homewrecker kneels at the end of the sandbar and washes herself over and over. When I am certain she feels absolutely clean, I let her have it. I roll her into the pool, where she becomes a ghost of the river trailing beautiful smoky cotton from a hole in her silly head.

It's such a relief. We never did need the social whirl. Tomorrow we'll shop for something nice, something you can count on to stand up.

There for a while it looked like the end.

DOGS

No one imagined how it would turn out for Howie Reed. But it all began when he was beaned at the rodeo picnic when the Jacquas, the Hatfields, and the Larrimores all thought that everyone was so sick and tired of having to clean up the fairgrounds that a game would be fun. Howie Reed got beaned in the first inning. It was softball and he didn't even fall down. At fifty-one, he was close to the average age of all the players. It was a stately game with no scores.

Right after that he went on a trip. He was gone for about two weeks, and just before returning, he called his friends to tell them he had walked into a door at the bank and blackened his eyes. When he got home the black eyes were almost gone. But it was clear that he hadn't walked into a glass door. Howie had

had his face lifted. It is not possible to really explain the effect on us, his old friends and acquaintances, of his new glossiness: the incisions behind the ears, the Polynesian serenity of his new gaze left many of our circle in Deadrock speechless.

The next time we all got together it was for a trout fry welcoming the new internist to town. In an area of long winters like ours, the entire community grows to hate all its professional people in about five years. A new doctor is taken in with urgent affection. The arrival of Dr. Kellman, fresh from the Indian Health Service at Wolf Point, was no exception. A horseshoe pitch was improvised; an extension cord was found so that a television set could be left running in the yard for guests following serials. Most of us drank and pitched horseshoes or skipped stones on the beautiful river. Howie fainted.

Dr. Kellman examined him and then came over to the carport where some of us had gone to avoid the sun. There, Dr. Kellman assured us that Howie was faking and that we should realize our friend was a mild hysteric; bring him a glass of water, possibly. Even accepting Dr. Kellman's diagnosis, it was awfully touching to see our old friend stretched out with his sleek new face aimed at heaven, the river flowing past him like time itself. In my view, it was either that very time, or the beaning, that explained Howie's face lift and faints. But that didn't lessen my concern for him.

No one noticed exactly when Howie left, but he was gone by the time the party wound down. And if there was any worry over him, it was lost in the uproar of the Kellmans' discovering that the thirteen-year-old corgi the doctor had owned since his medical school days was gone. Sylvan Lundstrom, who was everyone's lawyer and Johnny-on-the-spot, called the police, the sheriff, and the radio station, carefully describing a generic corgi from the Kellmans' American Kennel Club guide to breeds. It would be morning before we could reach the drivers'-training group at the school; they were usually most successful in finding lost dogs. Mrs. Kellman said she wished she knew less about the experimental purposes to which stray dogs were often put.

The dog was not found.

Monday I saw Howie in front of the Bar and Grill at the lunch hour. He was going out, I was going in. Howie is in insurance and busy as all get out, and a good kind of family man. So, the following seemed odd.

"You're on the phone with an old girlfriend," said Howie. "Your wife is at your elbow. Your heart is pounding. Your old girlfriend says, 'Just wanted to call and say I still love ya!' 'You too!' I shout like I'm closing on a huge policy. How much of this the old lady buys, I can't say." Howie shoots off with a little wave. I am not painting Howie as an ugly customer but as a troubled guy who didn't ever talk like this. It used to be you'd bump into him and he'd tell you something homely like the difference between whittling and carving (whittling you're not trying to make something). Now everything seemed so final.

Howie's wife went back to South Dakota in September, for good. To show he wasn't upset, Howie had his car painted JUST MARRIED. He went to a sales conference in Kansas City and forced a landing en route in Bismarck. He had to pay a huge fine for that, which he could certainly afford. But Dr. Kellman assured his new admirers that forcing a landing was a well-known thing disturbed people do. When Howie finally got to Kansas City, his company made him Salesman of the Year.

By October, Howie seemed completely his old self. The face finally seemed to be his own. His wife stayed away. We had another softball game after the fall rodeo. He was still driving the JUST MARRIED car and he was wearing a sweatshirt copy of the Shroud of Turin. He was all over the field and drove in four runs.

Dogs kept disappearing. It was making the paper. Dr.

Kellman was not building a practice as rapidly as he wished and he threw a Thanksgiving party, supposedly to introduce Diana, a yellow Labrador he had bought to replace the corgi. He said the corgi had left a hole in his heart that nothing could fill, but he let his pride in the new dog show. We all went to the party, even the other doctors. Howie was so disheveled-looking we asked if he was in disguise. "To be the leading adulterer in a small Montana town," he said mysteriously, "is to spend your life dodging bullets. It is the beautiful who suffer." His whiskers pressed through the taut skin of his face. For the moment of our nervousness, in the central-heating itch of fall's first frosts, it was as if the house were equipped with self-locking exits. We were quiet in the drifting cigarette smoke for just a moment, then went back to our carefree ways. Right out of the blue Howie added, "What the hell, I forgive you all. Everything I know I learned from Horatio Alger."

The dinner was served buffet style, and we ate with our plates in our laps. The Kellmans' new dog was beautifully trained and took hand signals, retrieving everything from black olives to ladies' pumps with a delicate mouth. When we'd nearly finished eating, Howie said to a young woman, a dental hygienist, in a voice all could hear, "That food was so bad I can't wait for it to become a turd and leave me."

Dr. Kellman diverted our attention by sending Diana on a blind retrieve into the bedroom. When she returned, Howie asked Kellman what he had to "shell out for the mutt." And so on, but it got worse. Spotting a pregnant brunette in her thirties, he said, "I see you've been fucking."

Mrs. Kellman tried to distract Howie by describing the problems she had had keeping the grosbeaks from running every other bird out of the feeder.

"You know what?" said Howie.

"What is that?"

"I wish you were better-looking," he said to Mrs. Kell-man.

"Get out now," said the doctor.

"Suits me," said Howie, once the mildest of our chums. "I've monkeyed around here long enough. I prefer white peo-ple." So Howie left and the party went on. Actually, the relief of Howie's departure contributed to its being such a terrific party. We all told stories that, for a change, weren't deftly to our own credit. I thought once or twice of making a plea for Howie—we'd been friends the longest—but thought better of it. Dr. Kellman had had to be restrained, once.

When the time came to go, it was discovered that Diana was missing. Mrs. Kellman cried and Dr. Kellman said, "I guess it's pretty clear that crazy son of a bitch has my dog."

In order to keep the police out of it, I agreed to go see Howie. At first I tried to get someone else to do it, but when I saw how anxious some of the others were to call in the authorities, I got a move on. He really had been a friend to all of us. But the pack instinct, whatever that is, was on alert. I think I felt a little of it myself, sort of like "Let's kill Howie."

Anyway, I made the feeling go away and drove up to Howie's house, a cedar-and-stone thing of the kind that went through here a while back. Diana met me at the door. Howie turned and wearily let me follow him inside. Various dogs gathered from the hallways and side room and joined us in the living room. Howie made drinks.

"I'm glad it's you," Howie said, handing me my Scotch. "The bubble had to break. Margie gone. Salesman of the Year. Every breed I ever dreamed of." He gestured sadly at our audience: Diana, a black Lab, an Irish setter of vacant charm, a dachshund, a few mixed-breeds who seemed to have a sheepdog as a common ancestor, all contented. And the old worn-out corgi.

"We didn't know what you were going through," I said. I didn't know who I meant by "we," except that I thought it was in the air when I left the party that we were pulling together over a common cause. "It started I guess when you got beaned." Howie looked at me for a long time.

"That wasn't it. I admit the beaning was what gave me the idea. I fell down to gain time to think. I lay there and thought about how happy I was that my marriage was on the rocks. The time had come to be off my rocker whether I felt like it or not. Margie had a guy but it wasn't enough. Then the company saying the future belonged to me. It was too much. I did the fainting business because I needed a jinx, I was superstitious. One thing led to another and I started grabbing dogs. It sounds crazy, but I felt like Balboa when he saw the Pacific. I'd never known anything like it. By the way, getting caught is no disgrace."

I took Diana down to the Kellmans, and Dr. Kellman, who is such a young man, made a seemingly prepared speech about how much Diana had cost and how in a practice that was starting slowly, you cannot imagine how slowly, Diana had been a crazy sacrifice both for himself and for Mrs. Kellman. Among the party guests there was the gloom of drama slipping away, of a return to the everyday.

In another two hours, I had restored each dog but one to its rightful owner. The doctor and his wife said they were glad to be shut of the arthritic toothless corgi, hinting it was Howie's punishment to keep it. Howie said it suited him fine.

Anyway, as things go, it just all blew over. And in fact, by spring, when Howie started having some chest pains, probably only from working too hard, he went to Dr. Kellman, joining our new doctor's rapidly growing list of devoted patients.

The schoolroom was small, and we had the same teacher all day long. You could smell the many coats that hung in the back of the room. The burr-headed boys sat on one side and the girls with their elaborate hair sat on the other. Between the two there was an idle hostility, which did not seem to have anything to do with sex but, rather, a plain and small hatred awaiting transmogrification and secrecy.

Our lunches were all stored on a table in black pails. We lived in such proximity and confinement that we had powerful attitudes about what constituted a proper lunch. Freakish lunches—imaginative preparation, ethnic hints, dainty wrappings—singled out the hapless owner as a pampered twit. I remember vividly how we silently accepted a trick miniature pie that was going the rounds of the grocery stores and could be eaten one-handed. A heartbeat from being singled out, each one of us seemed to arrive the same day with an identical pie.

That year, reproductions of Civil War forage caps, blue or gray with crossed sabers, came into our world. Every boy bought one. Just three boys got the rebel model, because where we lived, the indigenous saint was Abraham Lincoln and he took care of the slaveholders years ago, the men in gray. The three who bought the rebel model were the Emery brothers: Bill, Buck, and Dalton. They had nothing to do with the South. They were what was called common-ass hoodlums, who already had a running battle going with the game warden and a flourishing business in stolen hubcaps. But these hats drew the brothers close for the first time, and entirely away from the rest of us. Bill, the youngest, was thin and humorless and the most daring thief. Buck was feebleminded and got his crewcut by the calendar so he always looked the same. He didn't appear to have had the same mother as the other two. Dalton, ready to graduate, charming and crooked, was prison bound. When the Emerys found out about my big Lincoln log set, they decided I was the brains behind the Union forces, the men in blue.

When the school bus dropped us off that night, I took the route past the old stone quarry, a place we caught sunfish in summer. A path went around the back of the quarry, so close to the water you could see the shear of stone that dropped into vertical invisibility at the shore. I could see the Emerys drifting along slowly behind me, but I was sure I could make the shortcut to my house before they caught up to me. I was wrong; they made a rush and overwhelmed me at the edge of the sumac. Buck stood flat on the end of my foot while Dalton and Bill pushed me over backward.

My leg was in a cast for two months. But the torn ligaments didn't really heal until after summer began. My schoolwork suffered because the Emerys stared at me while I studied and asked to sign my cast, forcing me to refuse, making it appear that I was hostile toward them and the one causing all the trouble.

When my cast was cut off, my leg was thin and white. Across the windblown playground where deer tracks appeared in the muck, Buck Emery watched my crooked walk.

Buck often rode the bus with me, never taking his dark, stupid eyes off my face. His straight stiff hair was even and short. From any angle there was always a spot where you could see straight through to his white scalp, luminous under the hair with a gristly glow.

There was a sentimental attempt to rehabilitate Dalton in his last term at school. He was so clearly going to do badly in life because of his suave and malicious disposition that it seemed appropriate to put him in a position of authority. It was hoped that a day would come when he would not see petty theft or feeling up girls as the be-all and end-all he viewed them as now. The principal appointed him one of the safety-patrol boys and gave him the crossed white shoulder straps that identified the officers. He wore them with his Confederate forage cap and supervised the boarding and exit of the bus. One day when we stopped at the end of our road, he got off the bus with me and stared fixedly at my blue cap. He asked if I was still loyal to the boys in blue. I said that I was. But I knew he could see I was shaking. He said that if I was interested in my health, I would desert. As scared as I was, I thought of Abraham Lincoln and said, "Never."

"Have it your way."

My bedroom was an unfinished addition over the attached garage. The walls were made of what was called beaverboard. There was a window at the far end of the room and I could step through it into a huge, humid elm, go up and see the tops of the woods around us, or climb down into the yard. I had a crystal set in my room and spent long hours wearing the earphones, moving the whisker of wire over the nugget of crystal in its lead enclosure trying to catch the radio signals borne through the air around me. The room had no heat. Instead I had a thin electric blanket whose wires stood through the fabric like varicose veins. The blanket had a white plastic control with a wheel, numbered one through nine. In January, nine just got me through the night; by April I'd be down to four; then in October I'd start back up the dial again. I think the crystal set and the electric blanket supplied me with the largest general ideas about the world I would acquire in my grammar school years, vastly bigger than anything discovered in class, where the glacial communion of the three R's was held.

The last time that I used the five setting, Buck appeared in my window on a clear night and hung there, arms and legs spread to the corners of the window frame, wearing his cap and staring in at me in my bed. I didn't move throughout the long time he hung there, and I don't recall his climbing down. Instead, he seemed to disappear from the hypnotic center of the very fear I felt. I spent the rest of the night watching the same empty window in which I expected one day to see the atomic flash marking the end of the world.

Suddenly it was springtime. Frogs roared in the woods. Jack-in-the-pulpits sprang from black mucky soil in secret. Pike appeared from the big lake and sought the muddy canal that crossed our woods and swamps. I could see them from the high bank gulping water into their wolfish jaws and finning indolently beneath the undercut bank.

I started my paper route, learning all over again to put the three-way fold in the daily edition so it could be thrown like a piece of kindling. Among my newest subscribers were the

Emerys. "I didn't know they could read," said my father jauntily.

I delivered their paper first. It completely threw my route off. If I rolled my papers before school, I could deliver the Emerys' paper immediately after school was out and while they were still finishing the chores their father required of them. Their father was in "haulage," his term for intermittent employment. Chores in haulage might consist of stacking scrap iron or salvaged copper pipe, and it might mean cutting down a wild honey tree the old man had found in the woods while the boys were in school. The Emerys ran a line of muskrat snares and gigged bullfrogs. They could take a copperhead in their hands with impunity and make it strike through a piece of inner tube stretched across the mouth of a mason jar, spitting its poison inside. My father said that the Emerys had ability, which was his way of accounting for those who, though doomed, were undeserving of remorse.

Some days there were no chores. Bill, Buck, and Dalton would be lined up silently on the lawn. I pitched the paper, sailing it past their expressionless faces. Then I made off on my bike, putting all my weight on first one pedal, then the other.

Summer was making its way right over top of us. I played baseball after dinner, every one of the players sick on Red Man. I caught turtles. Because I hated books, my mother bribed me to read the Penrod stories and *The Master of Ballantrae*. Later, in the hope that I might be an entertainer, she drove me to play Mister Interlocutor in the annual minstrel show. Wearing a swallowtail coat, I read in a hysterical voice from cards she had typed, crazy questions to Mister Bones and others.

When the slow-moving green-to-brown water of the canal got warm enough, we swam in it. We drifted under the fallen trees that stretched over its mirror surface and caught the sunning turtles when they tumbled off. I had five of them, small painted and mud turtles whose cool weight in my hands and striving far-focused eyes thrilled me. The flare of shell, the arrangement of openings for head and legs, their symmetry and gleam of burnished camouflage were aching to comprehend. I took them to school and Dalton Emery, of the safety patrol, tossed them from the bus at forty miles an hour onto the paved road, where they blossomed red for one instant and flew apart. He pointed in his manual to a prohibition of pets on the school bus, an order of the state.

I didn't deliver papers that week. It seemed half the town called my father about it. I wouldn't explain myself; I guess I had the feeling that others might be listening. My father looked on in confusion as my paper route was turned over to an Estonian boy down the canal who had recently joined the Confederacy.

I had a path in the sumac that wound through low ground to a bank of cattails where redwing blackbirds flickered and sang. The maroon seeds had a salty taste, and to be undaunted by their rumored poison was part of the heroism of sojourning in the low ground. This same path crossed stands of milkweed with its pods of pagan silk and drew me close to the paper globes of hornets suspended in shadows. On the path I sometimes found a mother opossum with her infants stuck to her underside like stamps. The sumac path wound around and forked into itself. It seemed never to be the same from day to day. I now spent all my time in either the gravity of school supervision or close watching in my own home. My disappearances into the sumac were the only exception to all the unwelcome order.

I always wore my Federal cap on these junkets and carried a Barlow knife. I had wedged a piece of wood inside the knife that kept the blade point slightly exposed, so that it could be flicked open against the seam of my dungarees.

On the ninth of June, I placed my unsatisfactory report card on the kitchen table and headed for the sumac. I wandered down in it until I couldn't feel the heat of the sun but instead felt the cool breath of air from the mudbanks and sinkholes around me. A small hawk used my path for a whirling departure that cleared cobwebs at face level for fifty yards. At the first fork I found a snare that was meant for me. A powerful elm bough had been drawn down with a piece of old rope, the rope wound with vines, and the loop staked to the ground and covered with last year's brittle leaves. I tripped the snare with a stick, and the report of the bough carried through the bottom. I sat down and watched the rope snare turn in the air ten feet above me. In the climbing ground, I could hear the diminishing whisper of shrubs against pant legs. Then it was still.

I was taken prisoner the Fourth of July, a day that will live in infamy. My parents left for a long weekend on a cabin cruiser, which was really how summer always started for us, not flowers or south winds so much as cabin cruisers. The Emerys must have known because they took me right at the foot of our road. Dalton got my Barlow knife, and when we reached the canal, Bill threw my forage cap into the water and shot it full of holes with his twenty-two. I was held in a piano packing crate from Mr. Emery's haulage business.

"If you escape, we'll know where to find you," said Buck, with his way of looking through me. Buck was the one who would, years later, live alone with his father and help keep up the trap line. Dalton was in and out of prison. And Bill was killed in a rocket attack on the Mekong Delta. "If we have to go looking for you," Buck said, "we may finish you off." I know all this was talk, but there was something to Buck that lay outside of all agreements. He had shoved girls at school and disrupted the most official fire drills. No one used the drinking fountain without the fear that Buck Emery might push their teeth down on the chromium water jet.

"Just write a statement saying Abraham Lincoln was yellow and you go free," said Bill excitedly.

"But your knife is gone," said Dalton, "never to be seen again."

They left me with a pencil and a lined tablet in case I wanted to make a confession. I was given matches, a saucepan, a jug of water, and a box of Quaker Oats.

I saw the sun cross the sky and go into the swamp. The sound of frogs came up; not just the unpunctuated singing of the common green frogs but the abdominal bass of bullfrogs. The whippoorwills lasted an hour or two and the screech owls came out. A cold spring moon mounted high above the piano crate, and I fell asleep as its white light poured through the slats.

When I woke up, I was chilled deep down. It was just first light and Buck was staring in at me.

"Do any writing?"

"No, and I won't."

"It's your funeral," he said in his thudding way. He bent his face to better see me. Then he was gone.

I dumped the oats into the saucepan and let them soak while I pulled down rough handfuls of splinters from the crate for a cooking fire. I had to have this to do. I was frantic inside the small box, getting close to battering myself against its insides. The morning light glittered on the links of chain holding the crate shut, and the frogs were silent in the cold. My hand shook when I lit the matches, not so much because I was chilled, or that I could not repudiate Lincoln, but because the box had seemed to shrink to an intolerable size and my heart was trying to pound its way out of my chest. When the fire was going, I threw the gruel that was meant for my breakfast out of the box onto the ground. It dripped slow and cold from the chain while the tongue of fire reached out from the splinters. I tore more wood loose and threw it atop the fire, forcing the flames to the side of the box and wishing it were the battlements of Vicksburg with the slavers inside watching their kingdom fall. The smoke rolled over me and I grew faint. I remember thinking as I hovered between terror and opportunity that the sparks were like a shower of meteors on a winter night. I was quite certain I was burning up for glory.

The next thing I was in the Emery parlor, a plain room with antlers on the wall and a great painting of a waterfall so huge that the little tourists at its base seemed to cower at its majesty. I reeked of wood smoke. The stairs to the second floor went up at a steep angle like a ladder. The carpet runner was just nailed to the risers. There were a lot of chairs, no two alike. Bill, Buck, and Dalton were in three of these chairs and their father was standing over close to me where I was stretched out on the lumpy divan. Mr. Emery was little and hard and he had already cut a switch. He may very well have used it before I woke up, because the three looked like the most ordinary schoolboys you could picture. *I* was even scared of their old man.

I tried to tell from the way we walked as we went outside what he thought of me, but all I knew was that he was thinking, as we used to say, "in his mind." I caught a look of the boys watching. "They're not like you, are they," said Mr. Emery, almost to himself.

"No," I said, barely touching the word.

"They have to go and show off. I'm out of work, and the boys act like they wasn't all there."

I looked at the house. It seemed locked up like a dungeon.

"You'll always have something you can do," said Mr. Emery. He had a way of holding a cigarette between his thumb and forefinger and curling it in toward the palm of his hand. "My boys will go where they're kicked. Anyway, why don't you get out of here where I don't have to look at you. I won't tell nobody you tried to burn us out."

"Thank you," I said.

It was about a mile by car to the corrals and kennels. The trees were as tall as the pines in the North, maybe taller. But there was Spanish moss on them and on the cable guys that held up the telephone poles going along the road and turning up toward the house. Off to the north there were strips of lespedeza and partridge peas and some knocked-down field corn with crows flocking in it, tilting wedges of black in the autumn light. The weather that fall afternoon was still and warm, though the sun had the muted feeling of late in the year.

John Ray was waiting at the side of the corrals, a walking horse tied to an oak limb where he stood. He had called Jack at the dealership and given him the news of his mother. Jack had asked John Ray to get him a horse.

"I know you're shocked at me," Jack said, "but they can't get anyone out here for two hours, and I'm just not going to go up to that house."

John Ray always looked starchy in his khaki working clothes but he twisted around in them in a self-deprecatory way, as if to say that it was all one to him. There was a big bell on the side of the tack shed, and Jack asked him to ring it when the ambulance came.

"What did you find when you went up there?" Jack asked quietly.

"It wasn't no answer."

"So you just let yourself in?"

John Ray worked the bill of his cap in his fingers. "Yes, sir."

"Seem to go quietly?"

"I believe so, yes."

"In bed?"

"No, off in the side room there."

Jack looked over at the kennels. Pointers were jumping up and down the chain-link sides of it and barking. "Get Tess and Night for me, John, and I'll saddle up."

Jack went into the tack shed and pulled down an old worn trooper saddle with rings on it to tie canteens and check cords. There was a waterproof tied to it that hung down behind the stirrups like a shroud; dust had collected in the folds. Jack saddled the horse and put on its bridle. It was a great big, dignified-looking shooting horse with a roached mane and a long homely head like you saw in old cavalry pictures, a smooth-mouthed bay that had been branded by four or five owners. Jack thought that when the courts were done with the estate, when his sisters came down from Cincinnatti and his brother from Anchorage, this horse might collect some more brands.

John Ray brought Tess and Night on a forked check cord. The two lunged and stretched out on their hind legs as John Ray helped Jack tie the end of the check cord behind the saddle. The two dogs then jumped out in front of the horse at the end of the rope while Jack mounted and started down the road behind them. The dogs dug in and seemed to strive to tow the horse, who sauntered along, absorbing the jerks as he had done with hundreds of other broke and unbroke bird dogs in the course of acquiring the four or five brands on his hip.

Jack went about a half mile off the end of the road. There was an overgrown sorghum field that practically abutted a stand of longleaf pine, and beyond that it was all broken up little fields, some clearcut; and where it had grown brushy, the hedgerows were laced up shut with vines and brambles of kudzu and wild honeysuckle. It was still too green and early. Jack normally waited until it had frozen and the frost-killed foliage had dried in the cold, because the dogs couldn't smell as well when it lay on the ground and rotted.

Jack got down off the horse, which stood empty-saddled holding the straining dogs. He walked down the check cord and whoaed the two dogs, vaulting at the end of the rope toward the quail fields beyond. "Whoa, Tess," he said. "Whoa-up now, Night." The dogs stood on all fours staring ahead and, except for the trembling that shook them, did not move when Jack unsnapped their shackles. He made them stand while he coiled the check cord carefully and walked back to the horse and tied the coil to the back of the saddle. They continued to stand while he remounted and sat for a long moment looking down at the waiting dogs and finally said, in a long-drawn-out utterance, "All *right,* now."

The dogs shot off on separate but somehow communicating angles, tails popping, heads high, as they ran through a small field of partridge peas and wire grass and shoemaker berries.

They used up this field and cracked through a tall hedge, obliging Jack to canter along after them, losing them at the hedge and picking them up again in the next field, his shotgun slapping up under his left knee and coming out the far side with a strand of honeysuckle trailing from the trigger guard.

A big runoff ditch came up in the red soil, a place Jack normally rode out around, but he took it at a canter today and vaulted over it, seeing the big dark channel fly under him as he sailed into the rough growth. Jack thought about that ditch and wondered if he would jump it coming back. I'll jump it at great speed, he concluded.

When he came into the next field, the dogs were on point, Tess forward and Night behind at an angle, honoring. When Jack reined the bay past the low sun, the light flared red at the edge of the horse's nostrils. He stopped and got down, pulling the double-barreled gun from its scabbard, breaking and loading it while he kept one eye on the dogs. Night catwalked a couple of steps, and Jack made a low sound of disapproval in his throat and the dog stopped. Jack walked past the dogs, watching straight ahead for the covey rise. He presumed the birds were on the little elevation of ground under the old pines.

There were no birds. The dogs were still on point, and Jack pulled off his hat to run his hand across his forehead. He didn't understand it. He went back and stood next to Tess and tried to figure out what she was pointing. Both dogs were quick to honor any shape that might be another dog on point. He got down on one knee and saw the gravestones. Bird dogs back any white shape, and Tess and Night were absorbed in distant knowledge. Jack shouted at them and gestured harshly with the gun. "Get out!" he shouted, and the dogs cowered off and watched him. He got back on the horse and pointed out ahead. The dogs resumed, a little slow at first.

Jack felt the blood recede from his face. There had been

a community of tenant farmers here raising shade tobacco. The town was gone, the tobacco was gone, the church burned. Except for the graves, the people were altogether gone. Maybe they have heirs, he thought angrily, maybe they have rich sons of bitches living in Boca Raton.

There was a clear little swamp a mile or so farther on. It was circled by trees, and lily pads floated with their entirely green stems clearly visible for many feet underneath them. Quail had come out to feed, and the dogs pinned them down about forty yards south of it. Jack got down off his horse once again, prepared his gun, and walked the birds up. When the quail roared off, he dropped two of them. The rest of the covey made a whirling crescent into the trees. He tried to watch them down, at the same time calling Tess and Night in to retrieve— "Dead birds! Dead, Night; dead, Tess"—and, as they worked close, coursing over the ground the birds had fallen on, "Dayy-yid" and "Dead!" when Tess picked one up, and a triumphant "Dead!" when Night found the other and the two dogs brought them to hand.

He was sure he had watched the covey down fairly well when the bell began to ring, carrying pure as light turned to sound in the still trees. He stopped and gave it a listen. The music resumed and he felt its pressure, a pressure as irritating as a command to begin dancing. He climbed on the horse and reined him toward the down covey.

Then the bells came again, this time without any of their music, like a probe or like the light that went on in his office, in the roar of the air conditioner, that meant "Customer." I don't want this customer, he thought. He rode toward the swamp and felt a wave of courage that quickly receded. He wheeled the horse and yelled, "Tess, Night! Come here to me!" It's nearly dark, he thought, too dark to see that ditch. The dogs shot past, and in a moment he could not see them. He broke the horse into a rack until he saw the brush irrigated by the runoff. He pricked the horse lightly to set him up, released him, and felt as if he were going straight to heaven. The horse went down into the ditch, and Jack was knocked cold by impact as the horse scrambled without him, scared backward forty feet, and then turning to run home, dragging the broken reins.

He woke up in the ambulance. The driver was straight ahead of him, a black silhouette. The paramedic was next to him, a woman with a braid pinned up under a cap. Beside Jack was another figure, entirely covered.

"Don't drop me off first," he said.

"I'm sorry," the woman said, "but it is important that we drop you off first."

"I don't want to be dropped off first," said Jack.

"You we drop first," the woman said.

City lights licked across the two in front. They arose, penetrated the windshield, and passed. Jack tried to anticipate them, and once when the ambulance was flooded at a stoplight, he looked over.

They wheeled him inside. He was in a room that sounded like a lavatory. People walked around him. When a doctor put a needle in his arm, he explained, "I really didn't want them to drop me off first." And then it came, a miracle of boredom, and he was out.

This is kind of a one-horse town, and to get the fellows to stay on as directors of our credit union, we had to offer them a group life insurance plan and a few other things that struck them as the kind of perks people over in Billings were getting. The paperwork and physicals should have dicouraged everyone but they didn't; on top of that, the insurance company, knowing it was dealing with a handful of yahoos, required that we learn the latest in emergency procedures in the case of heart attack. We called a special meeting for this purpose, and it was at this meeting that my friend and fellow director Albert Buckland disgraced himself once and for all.

At the beginning of the meeting, Albert wasn't even there. Ejnar Madsen, a dryland wheat man from way off near Roy, managed to make it. Jack Dolan was there, winking at everyone from one side of the table, his Lucky Strike tilting a cone of smoke toward the big ventilator overhead. "What d'ya know?" he rasped at me when I came in. He sold cars, any cars, all across Montana. Beside him was an old sleepy man, practically a narcoleptic, named Dawson. Dawson never missed a meeting. His special area of interest was housing for railroaders. We called him Sleepy Dawson. Muriel Bizeau was there from the Chamber of Commerce. And Dan Pfeiffer from Taco Hut. The only one who had seemed to be unable to make it was Albert Buckland, who doesn't even have a job, having been born with a silver spoon in his mouth and spent his life hunting elk.

"Where's Albert?"

"Ain't here yet," said Ejnar, popping a breath mint.

"I guess we're gonna learn CPR," croaked Jack Dolan.

"What is it? What is that?" asked Sleepy Dawson.

"First aid for heart attacks," said Muriel Bizeau. Albert was also a park director, a hospital director, and a county commissioner. I guess it isn't fair to say he doesn't work.

Anyway, the CPR instructor arrived carrying his demonstration dummy. "I'm Ted Contway," he said. He was bright and looked committed to the day's lesson; he would remind you of a really enthusiastic pharmaceutical salesman or an aerobics instructor. He wasn't religious, but he was getting there. "I'm told we're missing one individual. However, I've got Lewis and Clark Rest Home at eleven. We better start." It was just as well Albert wasn't there. He chewed up guys like this and spit them out.

Ted Contway held his hands together as though in prayer, raised them, and touched their ends to his lips. He lowered his eyelids for a moment.

"In the course of this class, one of you could die of a heart attack. There is such a thing as first aid for heart attacks. That's nice, huh? We will learn that this morning. To begin with, I will discuss some general principles with you and I will ask you for a volunteer to try to put those principles into practice. Then we will learn correct rescue practices, okay?"

Suddenly, Albert Buckland slung himself into the doorway. He is a big dramatic-looking man, and he was dressed for a wonderful idea he had had the previous evening. He was still drunk. Ted Contway took one look and then made as though he hadn't seen him. Instead, he went to the other faces and studied each of them like a coach looking at his starting lineup. Jack Dolan's face disappeared behind a cloud of cigarette smoke.

"Cardio . . . pulmonary . . . resuscitation. CPR. Pharynx, larynx, trachea. Learn them. Ventilation, circulation. Not the same thing. Cardiac arrest. Brain damage. Death. The victim: stricken in a dental chair, up a telephone pole, in a stadium seat, anywhere. Things happen: minor things and deadly things. Is the victim, for instance, breathing. Is his blood circulating? We look at the beds of his fingernails. They are dark as night. Collapse of the heart, standstill, fibrillation. Direct inspection of the fibrillating heart reveals an organ that looks and feels like a bag of worms. Pain, bad pain, spreading from the center of the chest. *Fear.*" We all looked around at each other, trying to make a joke of this with our facial expressions. Albert Buckland wasn't really there as he ran his fingers down the length of his necktie and made it pop.

"At this point the alternative to correct and proper CPR is—guess what?—death. But let's wind back a sec to shock. Move your victim away from that object that got him. Victim is floating in a swimming pool next to a toaster. Stand on a dry spot and separate him from that toaster with a pole or a tennis racquet.

"Obstructed airways. Booze and dentures, a deadly combo. Rapid chewing, laughing, drinking, talking: the 'café coronary.' And old brother Death. Or: partial obstruction. Our boy sounds like a crow. Say to him, 'Can you speak?' And say it like this: 'Can you *speeeeak?*' Victim clutches neck. There's your answer. And now my dear rescuer, you are on your own. You don't have any of the goodies! You don't have the resuscitator, the inhalators, the oxygen. Rescuer, you are alone.

"Victim has both his hands on his throat. But maybe we know something. We go to our back blows, our manual thrusts. But death, my friends, is staring in the window. What if the victim is on the ground in shock? Can you turn him over as a unit? There are cuts on his face. Is his neck broken? You try artificial respiration, but you don't know how to do it right. When you blow into his mouth, you hear air escaping but you don't see the chest rise. Surprise! You've got a laryngectomy! Now what're you going to do? Maybe you don't inflate the lungs after a few tries but the stomach distends: a dead man can throw up on you! Maybe you're lucky, a couple of puffs and you feel the compliance of the victim's airway. You're a hero. You were lucky. But we are not talking about luck here today. We are talking about making life . . . resume."

With a sudden gesture, he sent the dummy floundering onto the floor. We were all in shock. And scared.

"Who would like to save this person who cannot speak, who cannot breathe, and whose heart is at a standstill?"

Albert Buckland stepped forward, pursing his lips and adjusting his pants.

"Ooh la la, is this what policemen and firemen do?" he asked.

Ted Contway, the instructor, smiled across the room at the assembled faces: half of them in the heart attack zone. Jack Dolan blew thoughtful plumes of deep lung smoke into the circle. He seemed to be in a rapture, as I was, thinking about —well, not being here anymore. Even though we all felt the drama of emergency, maybe we were hoping that Albert would louse things up and keep us from having to think about passing into the next world. At the same time, like in a play, we sort of believed in the dummy, which was a big rugged test item. We wanted the dummy to get better.

It was soon clear that Albert had managed to evade the general feeling. We could tell he thought this was a pretty dismal convocation. But he got right into it and straddled the dummy. "Don't despise me, love," he said. "I am but a man." In a heartbeat, his pants were down, and it was a trial for the rest of us to see who least wanted to watch the assault.

We all ran out of the room and clustered in the reception area with the secretaries. I think we were actually afraid of Ted Contway, who had been almost like a minister bringing word to us of something better. It was shocking that one of our group plan would have acted like this.

There was a disturbance, almost a scuffle, in the board-room. Albert Buckland came out in his overcoat and went straight through to the street. I tried to say something decent to Ted Contway when he came out. I told him that I thought we had all learned a lot. But he didn't hear me.

"I'd like a paper towel," he said. It was winter.

After lunch, I went over to my own office. I am a cattle trader and I was receiving a thousand head for a client's warm-up lot, and there was paperwork, mostly brucellosis, Bang's vaccination certificates, and brand inspections. Milk River range cattle going from the prairie to steroids to the fast-food lines.

Albert called me in midafternoon, and he was sober. "I got a room at the Murray," he said. "Someone called Diana and told her what I did. I got pitched out. You've got to go over for me. Diana likes you. She knows you've done crazy things but she likes you. She'll buy your story. Call me, I'll be right here."

There were narrow windows on the side of the Buckland front door. After the bell stopped ringing, the face of Diana appeared in the one on the right. She opened the door for me and I followed her into the drawing room. She sat down in a flamed silk armchair in the winter light that came through the curtain. Reflexively checking to see if I had tracked up the rug, I sat down and angled my Stetson between my knees.

"Where do I start?" I said. I could see she wasn't going to budge. Diana's features were immobilized and her mouth was a mark. I told her that no one wanted that class in the first place and that it had made everyone nervous. "Besides, we've all done things we wish we hadn't."

Diana adjusted her head in the light. The furnace turned on in the basement. I had this instant of hope that someone had pulled up. The curtains stirred faintly at the registers. Diana had not moved at all. I felt I couldn't really face the situation the instructor wanted us to believe in. Finally, there was a bit of movement, a focusing of Diana's gaze. She turned and looked straight at me.

"He fucked the dummy," she said. I stood and said I thought I had better go. She didn't respond to that. So, I went.

I called Albert, and he was drunk all over again.

"I didn't get anywhere."

"What did she say?"

"You don't want to know."

"Hm. You have time for a bite to eat?" I realized that there was a difference between eating and getting something in your stomach but I accepted. I think I was starting to be irked with Albert.

The Sport was crowded and we were lucky to get seated. There were four doctors at one table and next to them a crowd of merry ranchers from up the valley. Next to us were two handsome couples in their seventies. In their faces was this old-time social excitement.

Albert reeled to his chair, counting the house with a magnanimous gaze. He looked anesthetized. We sat down.

"Do you know," he said, "that I am the heir to Blair Castle in Scotland?"

"I didn't know that."

"I am the real Duke of Athole and a spurious cousin has stolen my castle."

"I see."

"*And no one in this dump knows it!*" he shouted. Heads jerked up. The Duke of Athole caught their faces and asked them if they even knew when Blair Castle was built. They didn't.

"*Twelve sixty-nine!*" he bayed, flagging the barmaid. We got in two orders at once. I should've cut him off, but the prospect of more liquor calmed him. When the drinks came, Albert drank his immediately. I was trying to think how to get out of this wreck when one of the couples at the adjoining table stood to go. The woman, perhaps seventy-five years old, had a full-length coat which my friend the Duke of Athole sought to help her with. He held it up like a bullfighter's cape.

"Why, thank you," she said and backed a bit toward the armholes. The Duke lost his balance slightly. It seemed that her attempts to backstroke into the coat only flushed the Duke in the opposite direction. By the time they crossed the restaurant in this way, the woman was frantic and the owner of the restaurant had Albert by the arm. I wished he'd have beaten him within an inch of his life.

"Give the lady her coat," said the owner, deftly trading him a drink. Albert downed it on his way back to the table. I hate discourtesy, and my appetite was shot. Albert stared at me from his secret place in the universe.

"I," he said, "am going to be sick." He got up and made his way to the rear, shoving people as he went. After a bit, I followed, hoping to find him dead, but instead I found him fervently embracing the base of the toilet, his chin on the seat. He was real sick.

I went back into the restaurant and got one of the doctors. I told him that Albert had a heart condition and that he was fibrillating to beat the band, on the verge of cardiac standstill. "Can you help?" I pleaded.

The paramedics wheeled Albert through the silent restaurant, those walls lit up over and over with the lights of the ambulance out front. When the gurney went past my table, I said to Albert, "If you have to go, go first class." I'd had enough. I called his wife and told her coldly that Albert had been taken to the emergency room at the hospital. She slammed down the phone in panic. It was as though someone or something had come between them, and this way they would get a chance to talk.

SPORTSMEN

We kept the perch we caught in a stone pool in front of the living-room window. An elm shaded the pool, and when the heavy drapes of the living room were drawn so that my mother could see the sheet music on the piano, the window reflected the barred shapes of the lake perch in the pool.

We caught them from the rocks on the edge of the lake, rocks that were submerged when the wakes of passing freighters hit the shore. From a distance, the freighters pushed a big swell in front of them without themselves seeming to move on the great flatness of the lake. My friend that year was a boy named Jimmy Meade, and he was learning to identify the vessel stacks of the freighters. We liked the Bob-Lo Line, Cleveland Cliffs, and Wyandotte Transportation with the red Indian tall on the sides of the stack. We looked for whalebacks and tankers and the laden ore ships and listened to the moaning signals from the horns as they carried over the water. The wakes of those freighters moved slowly toward the land along the unmoving surface of water. The wakes were the biggest feature out there, bigger than Canada behind them, which lay low and thin like the horizon itself.

Jimmy Meade and I were thirteen then. He had moved up from lower Ohio the previous winter, and I was fascinated by his almost southern accent. His father had an old pickup truck in a town that drove mostly sedans, and they had a big loose-limbed hound that seemed to stand for a distant, unpopulated place.

Hoods were beginning to appear in the school, beginning to grow drastic haircuts, wear Flagg Flyer shoes, and sing Gene Vincent songs. They hung inside their cars from the wind vanes and stared at the girls I had grown up with in an aspect of violence I had not known. They wolf-whistled. They laughed with their mouths wide open and their eyes glittering, and when they got into fights they used their feet. They spent their weekends at the drags in Flat Rock. Jimmy and I loved the water, but when the hoods came near it all they saw were the rubbers. We were downright afraid of the hoods, of how they acted, of the steel taps on their shoes, of the way they saw things, making us feel we would be crazy to ever cross them. We were sportsmen.

But then, we were lost in our plans. We planned to refurbish a Civil War rifle Jimmy's father owned. We were going to make an ice boat, a duck blind, and a fishing shanty. We were going to dig up an Indian mound, sell the artifacts, and buy a racing hydroplane that would throw a rooster tail five times its own length. But above all, we wanted to be duck hunters.

That August we were diving off the pilings near the entrance to the Thoroughfare Canal. We had talked about salvaging boats from the Black Friday storm of 1916 when the Bob-Lo steamer passed. The wash came in and sucked the water down around the pilings. Jimmy dove from the tallest one, arcing down the length of the creosoted spar into the green, clear water. And then he didn't come up. Not to begin with. When he did, the first thing that surfaced was the curve of his back, white and Ohio-looking in its oval of lake water. It was a back that was never to widen with muscle or stoop with worry because Jimmy had just then broken his neck. I remember getting him out on the gravel shore. He was wide awake and his eyes poured tears. His body shuddered continuously, and I recall his fingers fluttered on the stones with a kind of purpose. I had never heard sounds like that from his mouth in the thousands of hours we talked. I learned from a neighbor that my screams brought help and, similarly, I can't imagine what I would sound like screaming. Perhaps no one can.

My father decided that month that I was a worthless boy who blamed his troubles on outside events. He had quite a long theory about all of this, and hanging around on the lake or in the flat woods hunting rabbits with our twenty-twos substantiated that theory, I forget how. He found me a job over in Burr Oak cleaning die-cast aluminum molds with acid and a wire brush. That was the first time I had been around the country people who work in small factories across the nation. Once you get the gist of their ways, you can get along anyplace you go because they are everywhere and they are good people.

When I tried to call Jimmy Meade from Burr Oak his father said that he was unable to speak on the telephone: he was out of the hospital and would always be paralyzed. In his father's voice with its almost-southern Ohio accents, I could feel myself being made to know that though I had not done this to

99

Jimmy, I was there, and that there was villainy, somehow, in my escape. I really don't think I could have gotten out of the factory job without crossing my own father worse than I then dared. But it's true, I missed the early hospitalization of Jimmy and of course I had missed having that accident happen to me in the first place. I still couldn't picture Jimmy not able to move anything, to being kind of frozen where we left off.

I finished up in August and stayed in Sturgis for a couple of days in a boardinghouse run by an old woman and her sixty-year-old spinster daughter. I was so comfortable with them I found myself sitting in the front hall watching the street for prospective customers. I told them I was just a duck hunter. Like the factory people, they had once had a farm. After that, I went home to see Jimmy.

He lived in a small house on Macomb Street about a half mile from the hardware. There was a layout duck boat in the yard and quite a few cars parked around, hot rods mostly. What could have explained this attendance? Was it popularity? A strange feeling shot through me.

I went in the screen door on the side of the house, propped ajar with a brick. There were eight or ten people inside, boys and girls our own age. My first feeling, that I had come back from a factory job in another town with tales to tell, vanished and I was suddenly afraid of the people in the room, faster, tougher kids than Jimmy and I had known. There were open beer bottles on the tables, and the radio played hits.

Jimmy was in the corner where the light came through the screens from two directions. He was in a wheelchair, and his arms and legs had been neatly folded within the sides of the contraption. He had a ducktail haircut and a girl held a beer to his lips, then replaced it with a Camel in a fake pearl-and-ebony cigarette holder. His weight had halved and there were copper-colored shadows under his eyes. He looked like a modernized Station of the Cross.

When he began to talk, his Ohio accent was gone. How did that happen? Insurance was going to buy him a flathead Ford. "I'm going to chop and channel it," he said, "kick the frame, french the headlights, bullnose the hood, and lead the trunk." He stopped and twisted his face off to draw on the cigarette. "There's this hillbilly in Taylor Township who can roll and pleat the interior."

I didn't get the feeling he was particularly glad to see me. But what I did was just sit there and tough it out until the room got tense and people just began to pick up and go. That took no time at all: the boys crumpled beer cans in their fists conclusively. The girls smiled with their mouths open and snapped their eyes. Everyone knew something was fishy. They hadn't seen me around since the accident, and the question was, What was I doing there now?

"I seen a bunch of ducks moving," Jimmy said.

"I did too."

"Seen them from the house." Jimmy sucked on his cigarette. "Remember how old Minnow Milton used to shoot out of his boathouse when there was ducks?" Minnow Milton had lived in a floating house that had a trap attached to it from which he sold shiners for bait. The floating house was at the foot of Jimmy's road.

"Well, Minnow's no longer with us. And the old boat is just setting there doing nothing."

The next morning before daybreak, Jimmy and I were in Minnow Milton's living room with the lake slapping underneath and the sash thrown up. There were still old photographs of the Milton family on the walls. Minnow was a bachelor and no one had come for them. I had my father's twelve-gauge pump propped on the windowsill and I could see the blocks, the old Mason decoys, all canvasbacks, that I had set out beneath the window, thirty of them bobbing, wooden beaks to the wind, like steamboats viewed from a mile up. I really couldn't see Jimmy. I had wheeled him in terror down the gangplank and into the dark. I set the blocks in the dark and when I lit his cigarette, he stared down the length of the holder, intently, so I couldn't tell what he was thinking. I said, "What fun is there if you can't shoot?"

"Shoot," he said.

"I'm gonna shoot. I was just asking."

"You ain't got no ducks anyways."

That was true. But it didn't last. A cold wind came with daylight. A slight snow spit across the whitecaps. I saw a flight of mallards rocket over and disappear behind us. Then they reappeared and did the same thing again, right across the roof over our heads. When they came the third time, they set their wings and reached their feet through hundreds of feet of cold air toward the decoys. I killed two and let the wind blow them up against the floating house. Jimmy grinned from ear to ear.

I built a fire in Minnow Milton's old stove and cooked those ducks on a stick. I had to feed Jimmy off the point of my Barlow knife, but we ate two big ducks for breakfast and lunch at once. I stood the pump gun in the corner.

Tall columns of snow advanced toward us across the lake, and among them, right in among them, were ducks, some of everything, including the big canvasbacks that stirred us like old music. Buffleheads raced along the surface.

"Fork me some of that there duck meat," said Jimmy Meade in his Ohio voice.

We stared down from our house window as our decoys filled with ducks. The weather got so bad the ducks swam among the decoys without caring. After half a day we didn't know which was real and which was not. I wrapped Jimmy's blanket up under his chin.

"I hope those ducks keep on coming," he said. And they did. We were in a vast raft of ducks. We didn't leave until the earth had turned clean around and it was dark again.

David and Rita were starting their life together. David was a hard-working twenty-two-year-old with the strong features of his Norwegian parents and the muscles his manual work produced. Rita—a Miss Montana Runner-Up—was admired for her terrific ambition. They were married up the Valley in August and moved into the double-wide on Rita's father's ranch. Rita helped her father with the cows and the books, while David worked at the grain elevator in town. Rita wanted a house immediately and they had already saved for a down payment. When Mr. Penniman, the grocer, passed away, David approached the lawyer who was handling the estate, asking if he and Rita could buy the house. The lawyer, who was known all over Montana as a ladies' man, pulled his mouth to one side and gazed at the couple before answering. "There will have to be an appraisal."

"We know that," said David. He really didn't.

"And there is an heir, a daughter."

"Oh," said Rita. The lawyer, a Mr. Neville, looked at her. "She won't want that house. She's well off. But she may want a thing or two for sentimental reasons." She noticed how very thin and well-dressed Neville was, and there was something appealing about his sneering delivery when talking.

"We wouldn't mind," said Rita. David looked at her, curiously weighing her words. These domiciling arrangements seemed thunderous after an unexceptional small-town courtship. They looked at the house every day, a pretty white house that had been painted and fussed over all its life. When the appraisal came, David had to go home from the elevator, take a shower, change, and meet Rita at the bank. The bank officers went along with them, and they bought the house as is with the understanding that Mrs. Callahan, the grocer's daughter, could have a day in the house alone, to select mementos. There were beautiful things in every room. David and Rita packed the contents of the double-wide in the back of David's truck. Mrs. Callahan used a U-Haul and a crew to empty David and Rita's new home. Rita wept all the way back to the double-wide. That night Mrs. Callahan called to say there were no hard feelings.

Neville, the lawyer, phoned up the following morning in response to five panic messages from David and Rita. "You said you didn't mind her taking something for sentimental reasons."

"We didn't expect her to clean out the whole house," said David.

"You should have thought of that at the time," said the lawyer. "You bought it as is."

Rita got on the line and said, "She took the stove and refrigerator."

"Whatever," said Neville. "I've got calls waiting."

Neither David nor Rita could stop everything for this crisis. But it was a fact that they couldn't move into their new house until they had saved for furnishings. When David went back to the banker, he said, "I'm afraid you have been treated badly. But this can't be solved by me. You're going to have to learn this lesson and go on with your lives."

"So, we do nothing?"

"I tell you what. Why don't we try this. I'll wangle you an invitation for Mrs. Callahan's rodeo party. And you and the wife just put your best faces on and make a pitch to get your things back. Whether you do or not, you'll learn even more about life. Take it from your banker."

The night of the rodeo, David thought he was too tired to go. His muscles were sore from loading grain and salt and steel T-posts. But Rita was excited. David tried to be touched by her belief that they would get everything back. Even Rita's father thought that David would have to take on some of Rita's optimism and eye for the main chance if he was ever to get out of the elevator and go places. But he got dressed. So did Rita. By the time they put on their cowboy hats, they didn't know what to think. David took some aspirins and carried a beer to the truck.

They could hear the crowd roaring before they ever got there. There was a glow of light over the rodeo grounds. The bleachers were full and they had to edge their way past people's knees for a long way before they could sit down. They could see Mrs. Callahan and her companions in the reserved seats. Rita got cotton candy and visited school friends sitting all around them. David didn't want to move until after the saddle broncs. Before the calf roping, a man came onto the field and penned sheep with quick little collies on whose backs rode monkeys in cowboy suits. Rita sat back down with her cotton candy. "I can't believe her," she said, staring across at Mrs. Callahan and her friends, who now were leading a cheer for the dogs and monkeys. Then it started to rain hard. During the bulls, it became such a wallow, people headed for their cars. The roundup banners popped in the wind, and the hard beer drinkers got under the bleachers with their coats pulled up over their heads and jeered passersby.

Mrs. Callahan lived on the edge of town where it broke off into big pastures. Her place seemed almost like a ranch, with a few small buildings set away from a two-story gray house with white trim and big rose-cluttered trellises around the doors. There were a lot of cars parked in the driveway and in the yard; the rain-covered cars shone in the house lights. They were not really a cross section of the town's cars, and it made David nervous to be going in there at all. Rita, on the other hand, strode toward the house combatively. It got worse inside, where they could see their furniture scattered among the antiques. Everyone who David and Rita had ever consulted about their teeth or their bodies, their finances or legal matters, was there, gathered around a tank of Everclear punch. Dr. Dillingham went past, fastening hundred-dollar bills to his forehead with saliva, announcing, "This is how I meet girls in Las Vegas." When Mrs. Callahan doubled over with laughter, the lawyer Neville deftly spooned pickle relish into her hairdo. It went unnoticed.

Rita stretched out on one of the sofas that had come from her house. Mrs. Callahan waggled a finger in her face. "Keep it up," said Rita, "and I break it off." Mrs. Callahan moved her gaze to Neville and pulled the corners of her mouth up into a sort of smile.

Then the power went off for an hour. A few people walked outside with their drinks and waded in the irrigation ditch. When they came in, their muddy pant legs clung to their legs and they were all amorous. "Did you pull this?" Mrs. Callahan screeched at David on finding the relish in her hair. Now she was drunk.

"No, I did not."

"And you can steer the little woman right out of my sofa."

"Okay."

Harvey Perry, a sober accountant, led Mrs. Callahan by the elbow to the Mexican snacks, where her guests stood and stared in the anesthesia of the punch. Dr. Dillingham was on the phone with his bookie, holding up different numbers on the fingers of one hand while he placed bets. Mrs. Dillingham stood behind Mrs. Callahan in a wing chair, redoing Mrs. Callahan's hair with a brush and a piece of paper towel. Every now and then, Mrs. Callahan gripped the arms of the chair to twist in David's direction and fix him with a look.

The banker came in and played Garry Owen, the old cavalry call, on the bugle while two wives, making like vestal virgins, emptied a vessel of grain alcohol into the punch tank. Mrs. Callahan staggered out of the wing chair and cried, "The chili!" By the time she carried the big drip-baste pot to the table, there was an extraordinary tension about what the condition of the chili would actually be. Was it burned or dry? This was famous chili with cascabels and black olives, and woe betide if it had burned. But then, finally, it was okay, it was fine.

"You stay out of this," said Mrs. Callahan, shaking her ladle at David. The others lined up all the way to the porch. David got a beer, drank it down, and got another. He sat on the piano bench and listened in around him. A realtor, a rural type, picked at his chili, shuffled, raised his shoulders, and moved his lips real slow in an effort to be a man of few words. He was talking to Anita Baldich, the banker's wife. "I got this itty-bitty place on the edge of town," the pitch began. Mrs. Baldich had a sudden fullness around her mouth and her nostrils flared: a concealed yawn.

Meanwhile, Mrs. Callahan was telling of an out-of-body experience she'd had when she banged her head on a rafter as a girl. "Ever since then," she said, "I've seen life from a great distance, a great distance." David wondered if this was what had made her glom their furniture. "In effect," added Mrs. Callahan, "I died."

Said lawyer Neville, as though in reply, "I had an uncle who spoke with a Lebanese accent. As a joke. Gradually, he lost the ability to talk without his accent. My generation of people grew up referring to him as 'the old A-rab over the store.'"

"Oh, come on," said Mrs. Callahan, "don't cover up your origins for us."

"Easy there, Toots," said Neville. "You're letting the gin talk." Loud laughter broke out among the guests, really loud. Neville conducted the noise like an orchestra. The gambling doctor was particularly sarcastic in his laughter, and Mrs. Callahan hurled her bowl of chili in his face. That got it quiet.

"You carcass," said the doctor. "Remind me to do your next myelogram." He twisted his handkerchief around his forefinger and cleaned out his eye sockets.

David joined Rita on the sofa, but Mrs. Callahan spotted it. "Out!" she shouted. "Anyplace but that." They moved to the piano bench. "You'll regret coming around here," said Mrs. Callahan from her place in the next world.

Soledad came in at three to one, and the doctor raised his arms like a champ. "Stick with me, kids. What'd I tell you?" Mrs. Callahan patrolled the edge of the party loftily. Suddenly, Rita tackled her. People crowded around screaming. They were on the floor in a heap. The doctor got Rita and pried her loose.

"Call the police," said Neville in an even tone. David looked at his wife, more strange than anything in the *National*

Geographic, and felt a pride that surpassed anything he'd ever felt, a surprise that lasted long into that night, after they had lain down in the front room of the bare little home. He could hardly believe she was his. Her high, hard breasts were almost more than he could stand. The middle of her body was a blank in the dull light from the uncurtained windows, a blank except for the dark, precise crevice he ran his hand over until it seemed right. Then David got atop Rita. He had a horrifying picture of Mrs. Callahan peering in the window, but it passed in time for him to keep going until the emission. Later, he and Rita pondered what a climax for her would be like. She dabbed at herself with a towel. "I'd sure like to know," she said, and they went to sleep.

At three or so, the police came around and took Rita to jail. She went off with a red plaid wool shirt over her nightgown. David was paralyzed and helpless.

"You got her into this," said her father and made David sign an IOU for her bail. But Rita didn't get out till noon. Her name made the Courthouse Blotter before their marriage was even announced. Mrs. Callahan walked by the house wearing a neck brace. David and Rita went out to the ranch and walked over to the cows, who faced them with their calves behind them, slowly backing up.

"I wish we lived out here," said Rita.

"We don't."

"Get this," said Rita.

Rita's father called them by blowing the horn of his Ford a mile away. They ignored him and kept stewing. "I just wish we could enjoy our house," said David.

"The house. I just got out of jail." She snorted slightly. "The house."

"One word from your father about the good life on the ranch, and I break every bone in his body."

That night when Mrs. Callahan passed the front window, Rita called out from the sink, "I wish you were dead," David's respect for Rita's intransigence reached a point of fear. He suddenly felt less important in Rita's life than her quest for immediate justice.

"I feel like a second fiddle," he said.

"Oh, but you are."

"Why are you being sarcastic?"

"I wasn't being sarcastic. I'll fix that whore if it's the last thing I do." Now that things had grown so sanguinary, David pined for the sex schmaltz of their courtship. He stared listlessly in the mirror, remembering his grandmother telling him that those black pupils were the home of Emperor Worm. He was prepared to do a lot to get rid of this feeling, change zip codes, anything.

"If this is all too much for you," said Rita, staring into the sink, "get out of my way."

"I don't have to listen to this, he shot back," said David.

"You aren't funny."

"Get me out of this popstand, he pleaded," said David with no pleasure at all in his voice.

"The trouble with you, David, is you have no love of struggle."

Neville picked Rita up at seven to go over the details of her case. He was wearing a cashmere sweater, in a deep tomato. He repeatedly smiled like a dog snapping at flies on a hot summer day. The house seemed to arouse in him a meticulously subdued sense of hilarity. When they'd left, David made for himself a potful of corn on the cob, boiling it until it was done. He dumped the cobs into the sink and ate them as soon as they quit steaming. He went out to the truck and listened to the news of hostages and inflation. He turned to a country station and heard a rural quartet with a basso profundo who intoned love ballads like a professional moron. He imagined his and Rita's story blared by this sap and turned off the radio. He went back inside. He was nervous. He'd rather have had no furniture and no house than the current situation. He sat against the wall and read how to get rid of unwanted bikini hair once and for all, dead nervous. The next day when he got home from work, he found a note on the door. Rita was at the municipal pool. David went straight there in his overalls, covered with chaff and dust. He was breathless by the time he got to where Rita lay in a row of high school girls. When he spoke he was surprised at the pitch of his own voice. "Rita," he said, "I'd like to know what you're doing, what we're doing. What's the plan, what's the future, what is going to happen to us?" Rita angled her hand to make a little band of shadow over her eyes.

"I tell you what, David. I like it pretty well here by the pool."

They could set their clocks by the passing of Mrs. Callahan's humped figure. "Hasn't that thing healed yet?" yelled Rita from the doorway. They could just make out a streak of white against the viburnum.

"She'll see you in court," said David.

"Get off my case," said Rita.

Rita was found guilty of aggravated assault and fined. The court attached David's wages. Neville stopped by to pick up Rita wearing a smart Shetland, in lime. Rita went as she was. They were going to appeal. Rita's father came by with a card table and a standing lamp and a hall tree. They sat on the front stoop and drank beer. "I think me and Rita got problems," said David.

"Don't come crying to me."

They talked about farm price supports and the drought in eastern Montana. David could see the road like a band of silver. "What a mess this is, they all exclaimed," said David sadly.

"You don't sound so good yourself," said Rita's father.

The old rancher left a couple of hours before his daughter came home. When she returned, Rita put her foot through the screen. "God damn son of a bitch," she said.

"Rita, what's the matter?"

"I want a nice home, okay?"

"Okay."

"Whether you care to put your shoulder to the wheel or not." David thought she'd gotten this odd locution from Neville.

"But I'm actually paying for it," said David.

"Boola," said Rita, definitely from Neville.

At work, David tossed a fifty-pound block of iodized salt from the loading dock into the truck, and the rancher was out of the cab and in David's face in one second. "That could have gone right through the bed, my friend."

"I'm not your friend."

"What? I need to talk to someone about you."

At lunch the manager looked at David, exhaling cigarette smoke through his teeth. "I can't wait until your honeymoon is over," he said. "You ain't worth a shit."

"Fair enough."

When he got home, Rita's Runner-Up Miss Montana two-horse trailer was parked in front of the house. He undid his shirt and shook the loose hay out on the sidewalk. When he opened the door, it struck Rita's suitcase. She skitted out of the way and buttoned her western blouse over her tanned bosom.

"What I bought you is," she said, "a microwave."

"For what?"

"For batching it."

"For batching it? What is this?"

"And there's a big stack of dinners in the Igloo. We go to Helena to appeal. The state supreme court. Neville says we'll leave no stone unturned. We're going to bomb that whore back to the ice age."

"The ice age," said David, like a student in English-as-a-foreign-language. He thought of Mrs. Callahan stooped under the weight of her neck brace. She was impossible but she was all alone, while Rita and Neville had not only their enthusiasm but their goal of ruining her. David made a mental note to call the computer technician school and the Navy recruiter. Too, if he got away from the grain elevator, he could quit snoose. You couldn't dip and work on precision electronics at the same time. He thought of these possibilities with hatred, wondering if they had beaten the deadline for annulments.

David heard something outside and went to the window to see Neville hooking up the horse trailer to his Buick. He asked Rita what they needed the trailer for. For horses, she said. How were the horses needed in the appeal process? he wondered. For trail riding to keep their spirits up.

"I can hardly believe this is happening to me, he noticed," said David. Neville came in for the bags. Rita trotted to the car and that was that. In two days, she called to say that Helena wasn't buying her story. They were going to Elko to heal up, play the slots, get their minds off things. "They admitted it was a bad call," said Rita. "But they have to look out for each other. I can see where they're coming from."

"I can't."

"Don't."

Hearing that the marriage was shattered, Mrs. Callahan returned the furniture. She sent a note which made reference to the goodness of her heart. "I wanted," she wrote simply, "something to remember my father by."

PARTNERS

When Dean Robinson finally made partner at his law firm, his life changed. Edward Hooper, one of the older partners, did everything he could to make the transition easier. Between conferences and dinners with clients, the days of free-associating in his office seemed over for Dean.

"You're certainly making this painless," Dean told him one hot afternoon when a suffocating breeze moved from the high plains through the city. Dean had felt he ought to say something.

"An older lawyer did the same for me," said Edward.

"I hope I can thank you in some way," said Dean, concealing his boredom.

"I thanked mine," said Edward, "by being the first to

identify his senility and showing him the door. It was a mercy killing." Dean perked up at this.

Edward Hooper's caution and scholarly style were not Dean's. Yet Dean found himself studying him, noting the three-piece suits, the circular tortoiseshell glass, and the bulge of chest under the vest. It fascinated Dean that Edward's one escape from his work was not golf, not sailing or tennis, but the most vigorous kind of duck hunting, reclined in a lay-out boat with a hundred decoys, a shotgun in his arms and the spray turning to sleet around him. At Christmas, Edward gave the secretaries duck he smoked himself.

Friday evening, Edward caught Dean in the elevator. Edward wore a blue suit with a dark-blue silver-striped tie, and instead of a briefcase he carried an old-fashioned brown accordion file with a string tie. One side of the elevator was glass, affording a view of the edge of the city and the prairie beyond. Dean could imagine the aboriginal hunters out there and, in fact, he could almost picture Edward among them, avuncular, restrained, and armed. Grooved concrete shot past as they descended in the glass elevator. The door opened on a foyer almost a story and a half high with immense trees growing out of holes in the lobby floor.

"Here's the deal," said Edward, turning in the foyer to genially stop Dean's progress. He had a way of fingering the edge of Dean's coat as he thought. "One of my clients wants me for dinner tomorrow night. Terry Bidwell. He is the least fun of all, and I'd like you to walk through this with me. He's the biggest client we've got." Edward looked up from Dean's lapels to meet his eyes with his usual expression, which hovered between seriousness and mischief. For some reason, Dean felt something passing from Edward to himself.

"What do you see me doing?" Dean asked.

"I see you massaging this fellow's ego, forming a bond. It's shitwork."

"I'll be there," said Dean, thinking of his ticket to elevated parking. It occurred to him that being the only unmarried partner was part of his selection, part of his utility as a partner. But being singled out by the canny and dignified Edward Hooper was a pleasure in itself.

Dean left his car in town on Saturday night and rode out to the Bidwells' with Edward. The house was of recent construction, standing down in a cottonwood grove where the original ranch house must have been; the lawn was carefully mowed and clipped around the old horse corral and plank loading chute. There was a deep groove in the even grass where thousands of cattle had gone to slaughter in simpler times.

Dean and Edward stepped up to the door, Edward giving Dean a little thrust of the elbow as though to say, "Here goes," and knocked.

There came the barking of deep-throated dogs and the door parted, then opened, fully revealing Georgeanne Bidwell. She flung her arms around Dean, then held him away from her. She was an old girl friend, actually his favorite one.

"I can't believe it!"

"Neither can I," said Dean, feeling the absurdity of his subdued reply. Georgeanne, whom Dean had not seen in a decade, took him by the arm as though she needed it for support. "I haven't seen this man since spring break in nineteen-what."

Terry Bidwell appeared at the end of the front hall and blocked off most of its light. He took in his wife, clinging to Dean's arm. "A little wine," he said, "perhaps a couple of candles?"

Dean thrust out his free hand. "Dean Robinson," he said. "How do you do?"

"I'm getting there, pardner," said Terry Bidwell, looking at the hand and then taking it. Terry still seemed like the football star he had been. Georgeanne had always had a football player, and this was certainly the big one. His face was undisguised by its contemporary cherubic haircut, his thighs by his vast slacks. He smiled at Edward without shaking his hand and turned to lead them into the living room. Dean, behind him, marveled at the expanse of his back. But the face was most astonishing: handsome, it was nevertheless the face of a Visigoth.

A television glowed silently in the living room, running national news, and when the sports came on, Terry took a remote channel changer from his pocket, flipped on the volume, got the scores, and turned it down again. Terry didn't pour them drinks, but he went to the bottles and named off the brands. Then he went to the half-size refrigerator, pulled open the door, and said, "Ice."

"You've really made this place your own," Edward said, gazing around. Is that a compliment? Dean wondered.

"It is our own," said Terry. "I paid for it."

Edward turned to Dean, but without full eye contact. "Terry has an air charter service that fills a gap."

"The Northern Rockies?" said Terry. "A gap?" Terry's excitement over this point gave Dean a chance to look at Georgeanne, still as pretty as when they had dated. She had a long chestnut braid down the middle of her back and bright, black eyes that missed nothing. At one time, she had seemed to be astonished at everything she heard; it was part of her charm. That astonishment had been modulated to the point that it was now a mystery whether she was hearing any of this at all.

Seeing her took Dean back to when everything had seemed possible, though he remembered being exhausted by the alternatives. What was that old dilemma? Whether to cover yourself with glory or with flannel. I am well on my way, thought Dean, to covering myself with flannel.

They moved like a drill team to the dining room. Next to the table was a vast window with a white grid overlay to suggest multiple panes. A pond had been dug out and land-scaped, and the perfection of its grassy banks and evenly spaced, langorous willows depressed Dean. A silent woman in an apron began to serve the meal. Dean was in a swoon to find his old crush on Georgeanne still intact.

"Well," said Georgeanne, raising her glass. "How good to see everyone so healthy and so prosperous!" They all raised their glasses. The burgundy made red shadows on the table cloth. Dean had his throbbing hand on Georgeanne's leg. Edward stared at him and he removed it.

"You seem quiet," said Terry to Dean. I wonder if *he* noticed, Dean thought, looking back at the slab face with its small ears, and the corded neck set about with alpaca. He couldn't tell by looking over at Georgeanne, who seemed serene, practically sleepy.

"Dean has learned restraint since rising to partnership. It's very becoming."

"Partner!" said Georgeanne. Only a pretty woman could chance a screech like this one. Dean jumped.

"They've got me on a trial basis. I could be sent down any time."

"Oh, no, no, no," said Edward. "It's quite final. That's the charm."

"We haven't got titles in my racket," said Terry. "Just the balance sheet and a five-year plan."

Dean listened, nodding mechanically, and asked himself how Terry even got anyone to ride in his airplanes. He thought there would be a polite way to ask the question, but feared hearing all too clearly how America was beating a path to his hangar.

And he sensed something else: that Terry could be bridling at the idea that a smooth transition was underway here, from Edward, the firm's certified gray eminence, to a rising star whose performance might be limited by an on-the-job-training atmosphere. Even Dean couldn't guess how much of this might be true.

He dropped the thought because it led nowhere, and it was difficult to think of anything more than Georgeanne's leg, the yellow dress with its wet hand print.

Dinner seemed to go on and on, a less attractive form of nourishment, thought Dean, than an I.V. bottle. The work at hand was the airing of Terry's dream of "tying up the big open." When Dean raised his eyebrows slightly at this notion and looked across at Georgeanne, he realized she watched his lips, the very ones that had just said "big open," with rapture. He decided it was a smoke screen for the leg operation and drew them closer in complicity.

Nevertheless, this dinner where something was meant to happen, reminded Dean of his poor preparation for a life of enterprise. He had managed to reach maturity still thinking that you sat down to dinner only in order to get something to eat. Any kind of ceremony, it turned out, ruined his appetite. Like a child panicked by broccoli, he stole a glance at his unfinished meal.

Edward drove Dean back to his car in silence. It was late enough that the streets were quiet. Then, as if to emphasize his silence, Edward turned on the radio. When they got to Dean's car, Edward said, "You didn't do well, Dean." Edward's face looked very serious. "*And* you had your hand on the leg of the client's wife. Good night."

Dean was in shock. After he had let himself into his

apartment, he asked himself if he were crazy—he could think about nothing but Georgeanne and what he had viewed with pride as his courage that night—and decided that, well, maybe he was. He danced alone to Bob Marley's "Rebel Music." The weight of the partnership began to lift.

On Monday, it was certain there was awkwardness between Dean and Edward. It was equally certain to Dean that it was Edward's intention that this be so. They stopped outside the firm's library for the usual lighthearted word and Edward gave him, he thought, rather a look.

"How was your weekend?"

"It was all right," said Dean.

"Just all right?"

"Just all right, though it seemed improved once the part with your client was behind me."

"Terry is a good client," said Edward levelly.

"Is he," Dean stated.

The chill expanded from Edward to other key lawyers in three days. During that time Dean went from acute discomfort to a feeling of rebellion. He took Edward aside downstairs in the foyer. Dean was breathless with crazy courage.

"Edward," he said, "I'd like to see you retire. You're becoming petty."

"I get it now: you've gone crazy."

"Duck hunter."

Dean called Georgeanne from his office. "I still love you," he said.

"Is that so," she inquired. When he hung up the phone, it occurred to him that he was ruined. He called Edward's office.

"Edward, don't go around to your cronies and teach them to gaze at me like an undisciplined schoolboy. I don't enjoy it. Even though I'm a partner in the firm, it's taken all the strength

I possess to stay interested in this inane profession in the first place." Edward breathed on the other end in astonishment. Dean hung up.

Then he called Georgeanne again. This time he called her from the Bellevue Lunch—a lawyer's hangout—on a wall-mounted phone at the end of a long row of red-leatherette-and-chromium stools.

"Let's see each other right this minute," he said.

"All right." He could hear her backing up at his urgency. He offered up the idea that they drive down to the Indian Reservation. "At fairly high speed," he added, "then turn around and get back with room to spare."

They drove south to the reservation, a vast, mainly unpeopled area with scattered small impoverished ranches where four automotive hulks supplied spares for every running car. The awkwardness of a secret departure lasted for about ten miles. When they had dated, Georgeanne had been a precocious beauty, and Dean a confused and talented youth, planning to be a politician. He had just been kicked out of Alpha Tau Omega; she had just pledged Theta. She had stood him up for a linebacker and broken his heart.

When the linebacker was phased out they saw each other again but had changed to being friends. They had kept trying to flood themselves anew with romance in a spell of sex and courtship, but it failed absolutely.

Dean and Georgeanne recounted this period as they traveled the reservation, growing comfortable again.

"I just figured it out," said Dean in alarm.

"What?"

"We're friends, just good friends."

She looked out her window and stared at the elevation of an irrigation canal and the iron wings of a floodgate beyond.

Plovers hunted along the plowed ground, and the sky was extremely blue.

"I'm afraid you're right." The air whistled in the window vents. "We probably ought to start back."

After a mile or two, Georgeanne said, "A penny for your thoughts." Actually, Dean was thinking, for almost the first time, of what was implied by being any old lawyer in any old firm anywhere in the country.

"It's not going to work," he said. "Nice weather, though." Georgeanne quietly watched the prairie fly past.

They drove north to return. The country behind the city was flat, dry-land farm country, and the city when first seen looked like a sequence of grain elevators. As you closed in, the elevators turned out to be hotels and offices, really quite normal but for their isolation in space.

Dean drove Georgeanne straight to her house. The driveway ran up alongside a delivery door, providing a degree of privacy. Two flowering crab apple trees stood by the door, and the air was full of their smell and the sound of bees in their crooked branches.

When Dean got out to help Georgeanne with her door, Terry stepped up from somewhere and knocked him flat. The impact took a few moments to recede, at which point Dean realized he was on his back in the driveway. Terry opened the door to the house with one hand and shoved his wife through headlong with the other. I can call it attempted homicide, Dean thought, then negotiate an orderly retreat. He got to his feet and leaned on the car for a moment. His right cheekbone had swollen so that it stood out in his vision. Can this actually happen to a partner in a law firm, he wondered.

When his head cleared slightly, he staggered through the door with the most vitality and purpose he had felt in a long time. Terry stared at him in astonishment from the beside the refrigerator. Georgeanne stood nearby with her hands over her face. Dean tottered forward and struck Terry across the mouth with an open hand. Terry let him have it again, and Dean went down in a heap. He wasn't quite knocked out but he couldn't tell if he was alone in the kitchen or not. He gingerly felt the bone bridge of his nose and found it detached. He was face down in a fair amount of blood, and the desire to get away from that, as much as anything else, impelled him to get moving again.

He crossed a strangely quiet living room on all fours. He wanted to keep going rather than wait until he felt well enough to get to his feet. He could make out a small amount of sound, and he tracked it down a carpeted corridor to an open door. He crawled through that door and discovered Terry having sex with Georgeanne. He had her pinioned on a daybed, and his huge body jerked over her. Dean sprang on him and sank his teeth in his back. A shower of glass cascaded over Dean as his head struck the mirror. He heard Georgeanne's scream; then he went head first into the metal frame of the daybed and this time he was out. He was out for such a short time, his first thought on waking was to admire his own vigor. He had reached Georgeanne's house at 2:19, been knocked out and now almost fully recovered by—checking his watch—2:35. It had been years since he felt this good. He could hear an argument from elsewhere in the house, and it pleased him that Georgeanne was taking up for him.

He blotted the blood from his eye sockets with the draperies and looked around. He was in a kind of den with leather furniture, a globe, and a big glass ashtray in a wooden frame with a cork center for knocking pipe ashes loose. The blood spots on the draperies seemed to watch him.

The pain was going over him in waves. The light from

the window was clear and yellow and made him feel with sudden emotion the rarity of daily life, the wondrous speckling of the trivial, the small-but-necessary, and the tissue of small delusions that keep good people going.

He got up and went to the living room. Terry and Georgeanne were sitting on the sofa in an attitude that suggested peace was in the making. Georgeanne said peevishly, "Haven't you had enough?"

"Yes, I've had enough."

"I'm trying to persuade Terry about the truth of our relationship," she said, and, as a caution, "I believe I am getting somewhere."

"I don't think I can drive . . . myself home."

"We'll be right with you," said Terry. They leaned toward each other in a way that prevented Dean from hearing what they were saying, though he could tell he had brought them closer together. "Why don't we drive Dean to the hospital. I'll follow you."

Dean slumped in the front of his own car while Terry drove. Georgeanne led the way in their gleaming four-door along the crowded boulevard toward downtown. It was a shining fall day when the air of the countryside invaded the city. Dean did up his seat belt and gazed at the changing foliage.

"I hope this has been worth it to you, pardner," said Terry.

"It has," said Dean thickly. "It's opened up the future." His head nodded up and down as he confirmed this with himself.

Georgeanne stopped at the first intersection and Terry would have done the same, except that Dean reached his leg over and flattened the accelerator with his foot. They rear-ended Georgeanne in a grand splintering of safety glass and a thunder of metal like the rush of things in a vacuum. When all had come to a stop, Terry waved in the air toward Dean what were meant to be further blows but whose force was negligible because of the effects of the accident. "I hope Georgeanne is okay," said Dean wanly. His injuries had not been added to, but he was in great pain and overcome by the strangeness of his situation.

All three were taken to the hospital for observation, then released. Before they left, one young doctor took Dean aside and asked, "What is all this, anyway?"

"Well, it started out as a misunderstanding."

"Is it a ménage of trois?" asked the doctor. He cocked his head to one side as though the question arose from his love of science.

"No, doctor," said Dean, "but your vastly filthy mind has made me feel worse when I didn't think that was possible."

"You're on kind of a tear, aren't you. I wouldn't be smarting off if I were in your shape."

Dean went home.

The first day back at work, Edward asked to see him in his office. Dean was still widely bandaged, and he hoped Edward might pull up short of an actual inquisition. Dean's lips fluttered in a sudden exhalation.

"I was only going to suggest," said Edward, indicating a preferred chair to Dean with a broad open palm, "that if you were thinking of leaving the firm, this would be an admirable time."

Dean let out a brand-new guffaw. "Not thinking of it," he said, surprised at his own vigor.

"I see."

"Is there some sort of decertification procedure for new partners?"

"Dean, what happened? You snapped. Terry will probably take his business elsewhere."

"Good riddance. Less shitwork for you."

"And Georgeanne has aged ten years."

"It's about time." Dean was aware that Edward's face was moving toward him. It was hypnotic. Was Edward on his feet? Was his chair gliding? The face came forward, and as it did it grew more like a mask. The mask made a final and mythic ceremony of disappointment, an emotion too small to have ever held the attention of an important tribe. "You evil puke," said the mask. "We'll find a way to cut off your balls."

But something quite different began to happen. Word got out that Dean had stood up to his client. Evan Crow, an estate planner, seized Dean's hand silently one afternoon. And when Dean suggested the whole thing didn't sit very well with Edward Hooper, Evan got out his actuarial tables and, massaging the bridge of his nose, pointed out that Edward wouldn't live long enough to make his opinion matter. Other lawyers in the firm stopped by, leaned into his office doorway clutching papers, and winked or left brief encouraging words that could be reinterpreted in a pinch. "Giving my all for love," Dean reflected, "seems merely to have advanced my career."

Finally, he bumped into Hooper once again. "Edward," said Dean, speaking deliberately through his bandages. "I don't know if you realize how low the water supplies are in the prairie provinces. But in case you don't know or don't want to, let me tell you that the old potholes that made such a lovely nursery for waterfowl are very much dried up. Wheat farmers are draining the wetlands in the old duck factory."

"I don't get it."

"Do as you wish," Dean drawled. "But I think that it is very much in your best interests if you never shoot another duck."

Early one morning, before the coffee was made, before the messages from the day before were distributed through the offices and the informal chats had died out in the corridors,

Dean's phone rang. It was Edward Hooper. Dean hadn't talked to him in months.

"Can you come down?"

"Of course."

Dean had just put the jacket of his suit over the back of his chair. He started to put it back on but on second thought, ambled out the door toward Edward's office in his vest. He gave the closed door a single rap.

"Come in."

One hand in his pocket, he eased the door open. Edward was at his desk. Under a wall of antique duck decoys sat Terry Bidwell, elbows on the arms of a Windsor chair, fingers laced so that he could brace his front teeth on the balls of his thumbs. He seemed thoughtful. He tipped his face up and said, "How are you?"

"Never better," said Dean, "and you?"

"I'm fine, Dean."

Edward smiled with a vast owlish raising of his brows as if to say, "Where's the end to all this surprise?"

"Terry," said Edward measuredly, "asked to see you."

"My size has gotten to where I need to see everybody," Terry said.

"I'd heard you were clear up to Alberta," said Dean.

"And the desert the other way."

"How's Georgeanne?"

"She's off to the coast for a cooking seminar. Hunanese. And we bought us a little getaway in Arizona."

"All that cactus," Dean sighed.

"Let's come to order," Edward broke in. "I think Terry is looking for a little perspective on his air freight and charter service."

"No, Edward," said Terry patiently. "On everything."

"I mean that," said Edward.

"As in no-stone-unturned," said Terry. "Ed, try to stay one jump ahead of me, okay?"

"Okay," said Edward, looking into the papers in his lap.

"Instead of the other way around, Ed. Okay?"

Sometimes, Dean thought, silence can have such purity. It was so quiet in the room, like the silence of a house in winter when the furnace quits. Edward got to his feet slowly. He's going to leave this building, thought Dean.

Edward shaped and adjusted the papers in his hand. He looked at them and squared up their corners. He set them on the desk. He gave Terry a small, almost oriental smile. "Goodbye," he said, "you deserve each other." He sauntered out, his gait peculiarly loosened.

"I guess we'll have to take it from here," said Dean, feeling the solitude and bitter glory of the partnership.

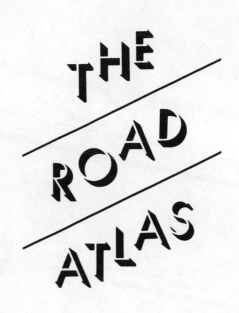

Across the way, a woman was posting the special in the window of the hotel. It was hot all along the street, and the sky was hazy from the evaporation of irrigated fields. Bill Berryhill came out of his brothers' office and looked for his car. He was wondering why he could not get through a common business discussion with them without talk of level playing fields, a smoking gun, a hand that would not tremble, who was on board and what was on line. When he got up from the table and said he had other things to do, Walter, the eldest brother, took the cold cigar from his lips and dangled it reflectively.

"Billy," he said, "this is a family. Without your interest we're clear to the axle. What are we going to do?"

Bill enjoyed the iridescence of this sort of thing and never meant to bring it to a stop. Walter was being a little bit dull, though, looking at Bill's eyes for his answer.

"I'm not a team player," said Bill. "It's sad, isn't it?"

The middle brother, John, wearing a bow tie and blazer, busied himself with papers, jerked his chin with a laugh.

"Where does that leave us?" John asked, clearly expecting no sane reply.

"You're going to have to thumb it in soft," said Bill.

Now he was looking for his car. He turned it up next to the hardware, a pink parking ticket fluttering under the windshield wiper. Beneath the other wiper blade, old tickets curled and weathered. The car, a Cadillac of a certain age, had a tall antenna on its roof. Inside, a big radio was bolted to the dash with galvanized brackets. Bill Berryhill relied on this for his cattle and commodity reports. On the back seat, a Border collie slept among receipts, mineral blocks, and rolls of barbed wire. He had a saddle in the trunk.

"I seem to lose my energy in those meetings," Bill thought. He fished a Milk Bone out of the glove box, and the Border collie got to her feet. "Here, Elaine," he said and reached it back. She snapped it away from him and he started the car. A glow of irrigation steam hung over everything. A breeze, an August breeze, would make it more comfortable but less beautiful. A woman ambled by, loosening the armholes of her wash dress. Bill angled the vent window at himself and drove through town, dialing at the big radio. He swept through the band before finding Omaha; he slumped down and took in the numbers.

He drove way out north of Deadrock and up through the sage flats to his trailer house, trying to hit the Maxwell House can with his snoose. The trailer sat on a flat of land under a bright white rim of rock. It seemed to belong there. There was a spring above the place, which Bill had improved with a screen box. There was a chain-link kennel that held his dogs, and a horse corral with shelters and a steel feeder for hay. He had his cutting horse in there and a using horse. The cutting horse was called Red Dust Number Seven and the using horse was called Louie Louie. There was a windowbox with some dope plants and a neat row of mountain ash around the front of the trailer. On the rimrock above the trailer sat the video dish, and it provided great reception for Bill's favorite shows: Wimbledon, the World Series, the Kentucky Derby, the American's Cup, prizefights, and elections. He went inside.

He turned on the Turner Superstation for the news loop and called Elizabeth on the phone, and asked her for lunch. He started a small sandwich assembly line. "As against apathy," he told himself, "I have the change of seasons, the flowing waters, the possible divestiture of my brothers." Bill had wanted a sensible mix of conservative investments he wouldn't have to think about. But John and Walter had got them into an RV distributor, a cow herd, a gasohol plant, and a grain elevator. Bill wasn't interested in these going concerns and he felt guilty about shirking all the fellow feeling. If only he could interest himself in keeping up with the Joneses, he could head off the cloudiness that troubled his days.

From the window over the sink, he could see two irrigators cross the hillside carrying rolled-up dams on their shoulders; the ends of the fabric blew in the drying wind. One man had a shovel, and a small red heeler dog bounced behind them. Maybe Elizabeth and I can make something out of all this, he thought.

Bill made the sandwiches. News briefs from the theater-sized screen threw parti-colored shadows around the trailer walls. Quarterlies piled by the recliner chair were wedged inside each other to mark the places Bill had left off. Elizabeth knocked on the door and came in. Bill was putting the lunch on the table. When she closed the door, the aluminum walls shook.

"How are you?"

"I'm great," she said. She was a strong-featured brunette in her late twenties. Her hands were coarsened by outside work, but it made her more attractive. She was a widow.

She came for lunch fairly often and sat right down and began eating. She and Bill both liked ice water, and Bill put a chiming pitcher of it on the table. He gazed around at the condiments.

"What do you want?"

"Oh, darling," he said.

"Come on."

"Hot sauce."

She reached him the Tabasco from behind the ice-water pitcher. They ate in relaxed silence. This is really nice, thought Bill. "I'm not getting anywhere with my brothers and it's my fault," he said.

"What are you trying to do?"

"I don't know, make a contribution. I'm just not a team player, and it's killing me."

"Why is it killing you? You're getting by."

"It's like not being able to get in the mood. I feel something is passing me up and I don't know what it is. John and Walter are so vigorous compared to me. I see my vital interests drifting into growth areas. It's platitudinous. I wish I could see myself as subsisting . . . tied to the land or some God damn thing."

"You need to be more romantic."

"I'm not romantic, am I?"

"Not about anything," Elizabeth said. "It's your highest limitation."

"I know you're right," said Bill. "But God damn it, this

is Big Sky country, this is the American West. It shouldn't be a problem."

"It's a problem if you're so defeated by it."

Bill wished they could make love after lunch. All energy would pass to his abdominal nerves. But it was out of the question. Volition would fill the air. And it seemed he didn't want that.

Bill and Elizabeth had a lot in common, not as much as Bill would wish, but many things: a love of reading, a wryness, superfluous lives on land that had gone up in value while losing its utility. It could seem to him that her bereavement was her real location. She sustained in her actual home the air of a life lived elsewhere just as Bill's education had removed him. More than that, they faced lives that could be behind them. Bill thought that while it terrified him, it might well have consoled Elizabeth to know that the struggle for love and wholeness did not have to be gone through again. He even thought it was mean-spirited to view her beauty and merit as something wasted because it was not offered up to use. Still, all these considerations produced cloudiness and an irresolute foreground.

"I met a girl at that little gift shop who wanted to meet you. Karen. Said she could come out. I'm sure she'll sleep with you."

"I'll have to look into it," Bill said wanly. His brothers weren't like this. They'd show merriment for Karen. They'd want to get them a little and not think it over. Bill reached across and took Elizabeth's hand. It was strong. It weighed something. He wished she wouldn't smile when she looked at him. She wasn't pornographic. Sometimes when he went volitionless, her eyes glittered as though a little victory were at hand. What victory? Watching someone pull himself out of a hole?

A small cloudburst hit the trailer, the kind you can see all the way around in the mountains. Bill got up to look out. It hit so suddenly that the drops of water threw dust in the air. His two horses swiveled their butts into the wind, and their tails blew up along their flanks. Then it stopped and Bill opened the door to let the air, fragrant with cedar, fill the trailer. He sat down and refilled their ice water.

"Let's do something this year. I feel my life is almost over," Bill said.

"You always feel your life is almost over. What do you want to do?"

"I'd like to go to Monticello," said Bill. But suddenly he could not understand why it had to be impossible for him and Elizabeth to be happy in an ordinary way. Then it subsided.

"Why don't we make a real trip," he said. "We'll take the horses and go to Texas. That'll get us south and sort of east. We'll be almost there."

"The Texans will be funny. We can go to the Alamo."

"If it's all right, I'd like to visit Bunker Hill."

"Then let's leave our horses at home."

"I don't feel like eating," said Bill.

"I really can't appeal to your needs, can I?" said Elizabeth.

But as the days went by, the trip did acquire some actuality. They bought a road atlas, even though Bill had often said the road atlas had ruined American life. But the road atlas made it clear that their trip was pretty much of a zigzag. Still, they spent frequent evenings in the trailer foreseeing the meaning of their destinations.

John and Walter asked if they could all have a drink at the hotel. When they got there, Bill was already seated next to the pensioners in the lobby. An old cowboy with a tray bolted to his electric wheelchair shot in and out of the bar delivering drinks. The three sat around a table that gave them some distance from others and moved their whiskey thoughtfully on coasters like Ouija styluses. John produced a sentimental appearance in his bow tie, his hair parted closer to the crown than was currently fashionable. Walter, astonished gull–wing eyebrows and dark jowls, looked the power broker he was with his wide tie and grim suit. They weren't such bad fellows, Bill thought. They have the advantage of the here and now, and Bill was man enough not to blame his slipping gears on them.

"What's the deal on the cows?" Walter asked.

"I'm going to can about thirty head."

"How come?"

"Old, dry."

"Ship all the steer calves?"

"I don't think so," Bill said. "The market's not very good, but it has to get some better. Fifty-five counties in drought relief. A lot of cattle went through early. It'll come back a little by fall. But I want to hold the heifers over and sell them as replacements. I don't see two droughts in a row."

"It could happen," said John wisely. He reset his glasses with thumb and forefinger, then squeezed the wings of his nose.

"It could happen," Bill repeated.

"What'll you do after you ship? You going to feed them yourself?" Walter said with an ironic smile.

"No, Walter. I'm going to hire that out," Bill almost shouted.

"Easy, big feller," said Walter. "Be cool."

"Refill?" asked John, holding his arm up. A little circular gesture told the old cowboy to scoot into the atmospheric lighting of the bar. John began to talk with his air of halting introspection. He was very likely to say something specious, but the appearance of its having been tugged from the depths of consideration made him difficult to contradict.

"Walt and I have been kind of forging ahead all year as though we had your proxy."

"So you have," Bill said. He gave a vast sigh.

"We take it that things can't stagnate altogether and the day will come when you'll want to take ahold, but that day is not here now."

"That sort of describes it," Bill said. "And it sort of doesn't. I see the three of us as being fortunate, don't you?"

"What we have long understood," said Walter, "is that you feel a mandate for greater meaning, and we don't oppose that. John and me are just two little old MBAs. We want more of what we've got, and we're too old to change. When we get this thing right, we—or one of us—might run for office. That's where significance as we see it kicks in."

"But," John cut in, "by way of reassuring you, Bill. We're thriving on all the fronts we have chosen to fight on."

"What about the gasohol plant?"

"We dialed it down to an enriched feeder deal. The pig guys are knocking our door down."

"I thought maybe you trapped yourself there."

"Did not."

Superfluously, Bill thought of the cleverness of the pig, his rambling ways. Gasohol was cloudy, pig feed clear. Drink Two permitted him to ask, "Do you want to buy me out?"

"Not necessarily," said John, indenting the bows of his tie.

"In other words, we could disagree about valuation."

As soon as John began to demur, sinking his chin into the softness of his neck, Walter cut across and said, "Let's say that's the case."

"Ten times earnings," Bill said.

John's and Walter's disparaging chuckles were hair-trigger affairs that gave them away better than anything Bill could have made up. Bill saw himself as Jefferson while John and Walter were the twin halves of Hamilton's brain.

"Come on, you crooks, give me a number," said Bill, and his brothers raised their eyes to the plaster ceiling. Just then, Bill felt a gust of power in the room, a brief touch of the thing that held these men's interest, and he did not necessarily despise it any more than he would despise weather. If he ever worked it out with Elizabeth, he might not want to have mishandled this.

"The trouble with this sort of thing," said Bill, "is you never know who the Honest Johns are, do you? I mean, we hang it on profits, and the company suddenly goes into a long-range development plan and the profits go down."

Walter was hot. "How do you go into long-range development retailing RVs and selling pig feed?"

"You'd find a way," said Bill.

Before things got out of hand, John spoke up. "You've got the performance to date. Our little-bitty deal couldn't stand hostility. We could never move around with that hanging over us."

"Rest assured the cows aren't going into long-range development," said Bill. "I'm holding my end down."

"Don't be a son of a bitch," said Walter. Walter didn't give a damn right now and you had to listen to him.

"It's clear the both of you view me as a remittance man. An interference."

"No, we don't," John chimed in. "But your search for meaning is a bore."

Bill felt trapped by the characterization. These brutes were sincere. Walter and John got to their feet. This was going nowhere. "Go fuck yourselves," said Bill.

"*You* go fuck *your*self," said John.

"I see your point," said Bill.

In despair over all this, Bill went to the gift shop and

introduced himself to Karen, who was busy signing Italian pottery that had come in without pedigree from the sheds of Missoula. He supplied her with imaginary Tuscan monikers while she endorsed the bottoms with a little paintbrush. By the time she got through the ashtrays and vast number of coffee mugs, they were great friends. They had lunch at the B & G and had a quick "my place or your place" conversation while Bill scrutinized her through the smoke of his Camels.

"I don't know anyone who still smokes," she said.

"I'm very ancient in my ways," said Bill, paralyzed by ennui. An hour later, they had gone from a comfortable missionary position to the kind of three-point stance used by football players. After making love, he had a spell of dullness like the two weeks that make the difference between a bad and a good haircut. As Bill drove off he thought, I hope I get the clap. I've betrayed the only woman who means anything to me.

Bill had hired an acid casualty to feed cattle for him, an ideal hand who never looked to the right or the left and kept his mind firmly on a job it was very hard for most people to keep their minds on. He called himself Waylon Remington, though Bill was quite sure that was not really his name. All that was left of Waylon's hairdo from the good-time days was a long goatee. He talked to himself.

It had taken Bill a long time to get used to lining Waylon Remington out on a job. He would give Waylon his instructions and get no reaction whatsoever. It was fairly disconcerting until Bill realized that Waylon heard him perfectly well and would act as instructed. But Bill felt very solitary telling him what to do as though making a speech in an empty room.

Today, he explained to Waylon Remington how he wanted his stack yard arranged. "Just get the big hay panels from near the house and wire them up in a square around the stack. Make sure your entryway is on level ground so you can get in and out with the tractor" Bill and Waylon were driving down through the hay meadow as Bill spoke. "And use plenty of steel stakes on those panels around the entry, or the whole shitaree will fall down. Remember you have to drive that tractor all the way around the stack to get ahold of the round bales." Waylon Remington stared at the hood ornament.

"Now," said Bill as they reached the irrigation headgate, "let's get out here." The two got out and went to the flume. It was about half full. The water took off toward the south, split up a couple of times, and fanned onto the field. "Now, Waylon." Bill glanced over at Waylon Remington, just two feet away. His mouth was open and Bill could hear the breath in his teeth; his lower lip was cracked and dry. "I need for you to be moving those dams just once a day from now on because we're starting to lose our water for the year. Keep moving them twelve steps at a time but once a day instead of three."

He went down alongside the Parshall flume. "Keep track of these numbers on the gauge. If you see a big change, either up or down, come get me and we'll read the tables and make another plan. You never know when they'll shut down the center pivots upstream. So, it could change. . . . Waylon?"

Bill wanted to get the horses but he wasn't confident Waylon could keep a horse moving; so he put the truck into four-wheel drive and took him around four or five more projects. Tighten about a mile and a half of fence, adding clips and stays as he went. Fix the chain in the manure spreader. Add hydraulic fluid to the front-end loader and hit all the grease points. They drove past the salt blocks set out in old tractor tires, checked fly rubs, tanks, and springs. This didn't require Bill to talk, and it got pretty quiet in the cab. Then Waylon Remington began to hum. He hummed songs from Jefferson Airplane. Bill began to panic. Could he really leave?

Bill put five yearlings into the pen and warmed up Red Dust Number Seven in front of them. The young horse was cinchy and liable to buck the first few minutes. He stopped him and rolled him back a couple of times.

Bill trotted Red in a circle. He had him in a twisted wire snaffle and draw reins, and he kept Red's head just flexed enough that he could see the glint of his eye on the inside of the circle. Red was getting so that if Bill took a deep seat and moved his feet forward in the stirrups he would start down into his stop. Then he'd likely as not run his head up and be piggy about turning. This was where Bill thought he was the roughest. Red kind of straightened up when he had a cow in front of him.

Bill cut a yearling out of the small herd. The steer just stopped and took things in. The steer moved and Red boiled over, squealing and running off. Bill took a light hold of him, rode him in a big circle, then back to the same place on the steer. This time, Red lowered himself and waited; and when the cow moved he sat right hard on his hocks, broke off, stopped hard, and came back inside the cow. Now he was working, his ears forward, his eyes bright. This little horse was such a cow horse, he sometimes couldn't stand the pressure he put on himself. The steer then threw a number nine in his tail and bolted. Red stopped it right in front of the herd. He was low all over, ready to move anywhere. Bill tipped his head and saw the glint of eye and the bright flare at his nostrils. Bill cut another cow.

This one traveled more and let Bill free Red, moving fast across the pen. Bill was pleased to be reminded that this was a horse you could call on and use. After a minute more, Red was blowing and Bill put his hand down on his neck to release him.

The colt's head came up as though he were emerging from a dream, and he looked around.

First, they were going to drive, then a nervousness about being gone so long came over them. Bill said, "Why are we going on this trip anyway?"

"I wanted to go to the Alamo, and then you wanted to go to Monticello, I think, and Bunker Hill."

"What happened to that?"

"You said the Texans would be funny and let's skip Texas. And then we were going to go—I don't know, something about Thomas Jefferson."

"That seems inappropriate. We'd spend the whole time explaining to strangers what we were doing."

"Well, we'll just go somewhere else," Elizabeth said. She was looking long and hard at Bill, who was clearly in some kind of turmoil. He knew that, even while they talked, his brothers were making things happen. Bill didn't seem to want what he and his brothers owned, but he didn't want it taken away.

"I don't know about Monticello," he said. "It's just a big house. The Alamo and Bunker Hill speak for themselves."

"Oh, Bill."

Bill felt serious failure very close now.

"Listen," she said, "I'm going to take this trip." In her green cotton shirt, she seemed mighty. Bill didn't say anything.

"You ought to come, Bill. But I'm beginning to think you won't."

"I'm going to miss you."

"I'm going to take the road atlas."

"You think I've just quit, don't you?"

"I don't know whether you have or not," she said. "But I can't. Something's got to give."

FLIGHT

During bird season, dogs circle each other in my kitchen, shell vests are piled in the mudroom, all drains are clogged with feathers, and hunters work up hangover remedies at the icebox. As a diurnal man, I gloat at these presences, estimating who will and who will not shoot well.

This year was slightly different in that Dan Ashaway arrived seriously ill. Yet this morning, he was nearly the only clear-eyed man in the kitchen. He helped make the vast breakfast of grouse hash, eggs, juice, and coffee. Bill Upton and his brother, Jerry, who were miserable, loaded dogs and made a penitentially early start. I pushed away some dishes and lit a breakfast cigar. Dan refilled our coffee and sat down. We've hunted birds together for years. I live here and Dan flies in from Philadelphia. Anyway, this seemed like the moment.

"How bad off are you?" I asked.

"I'm afraid I'm not going to get well," said Dan directly, shrugging and dropping his hands to the arms of his chair. That was that. "Let's get started."

We took Dan's dogs at his insistence. They jumped into the aluminum boxes on the back of the truck when he said "Load": Betty, a liver-and-white female, and Sally, a small bitch with a banded face. These were—I should say *are*—two dead-broke pointers who found birds and retrieved without much handling. Dan didn't even own a whistle.

As we drove toward Roundup, the entire pressure of my thoughts was of how remarkable it was to be alive. It seemed a strange and merry realization.

The dogs rode so quietly I had occasion to remember when Betty was a pup and yodeled in her box, drawing stares in all the towns. Since then she had quieted down and grown solid at her job. She and Sally had hunted everywhere from Albany, Georgia, to Wilsall, Montana. Sally was born broke but Betty had the better nose.

We drove between two ranges of desertic mountains, low ranges without snow or evergreens. Section fences climbed infrequently and disappeared over the top or into blue sky. There was one little band of cattle trailed by a cowboy and a dog, the only signs of life. Dan was pressing sixteen-gauge shells into the elastic loops of his cartridge belt. He was wearing blue policeman's suspenders and a brown felt hat, a businessman's worn-out Dobbs.

We watched a harrier course the ground under a bluff, sharptail grouse jumping in his wake. The harrier missed a half dozen, wheeled on one wingtip, and nailed a bird in a pop of down and feathers. As we resumed driving, the hawk was hooded over its prey, stripping meat from the breast.

Every time the dirt road climbed to a new vantage point, the country changed. For a long time, a green creek in a tunnel of willows was alongside us; then it went off under a bridge, and we climbed away to the north. When we came out of the low ground, there seemed no end to the country before us: a great wide prairie with contours as unquestionable as the sea. There were buttes pried up from its surface and yawning coulees with streaks of brush where the springs were. We had to abandon logic to stop and leave the truck behind. Dan beamed and said, "Here's the spot for a big nap." The remark frightened me.

"Have we crossed the stagecoach road?" Dan asked.

"Couple miles back."

"Where did we jump all those sage hens in 1965?"

"Right where the stagecoach road passed the old hotel."

Dan had awarded himself a little English sixteen-gauge for graduating from the Wharton School of Finance that year. It was in the gun rack behind our heads now, the bluing gone and its hinge pin shot loose.

"It's a wonder we found anything," said Dan from afar, "with the kind of run-off dog we had. Señor Jack. You had to preach religion to Señor Jack every hundred yards or he'd leave us. Remember? It's a wonder we fed that common bastard." Señor Jack was a dog with no talent, loyalty, or affection, a dog we swore would drive us to racquet sports. Dan gave him away in Georgia.

"He found the sage hens."

"But when we got on the back side of the Little Snowies, remember? He went right through all those sharptails like a train. We should have had deer rifles. A real wonder dog. I wonder where he is. I wonder what he's doing. Well, it's all an illusion, a very beautiful illusion, a miracle which is taking place before our very eyes. 1965. I'll be damned."

The stagecoach road came in around from the east again, and we stopped: two modest ruts heading into the hills. We released the dogs and followed the road around for half an hour. It took us past an old buffalo wallow filled with water. Some teal got up into the wind and wheeled off over the prairie.

About a mile later the dogs went on point. It was hard to say who struck game and who backed. Sally catwalked a little, relocated, and stopped; then Betty honored her point. So we knew we had moving birds and got up on them fast. The dogs stayed staunch, and the long covey rise went off like something tearing. I killed a going-away and Dan made a clean left and right. It was nice to be reminded of his strong heads-up shooting. I always crawled all over my gun and lost some quickness. It came of too much waterfowling when I was young. Dan had never really been out of the uplands and had speed to show for it.

Betty and Sally picked up the birds; they came back with eyes crinkled, grouse in their mouths. They dropped the birds and Dan caught Sally with a finger through her collar. Betty shot back for the last bird. She was the better marking dog.

We shot another brace in a ravine. The dogs pointed shoulder to shoulder and the birds towered. We retrieved those, walked up a single, and headed for a hillside spring with a bar of bright buckbrush, where we nooned up with the dogs. The pretty bitches put their noses in the cold water and lifted their heads to smile when they got out of breath drinking. Then they pitched down for a rest. We broke the guns open and set them out of the way. I laid a piece of paper down and arranged some sandwiches and tangy apples from my own tree. We stretched out on one elbow, ate with a free hand, and looked off over the prairie, to me the most beautiful thing in the world. I wish I could see all the grasslands, while we still have them.

Then I couldn't stand it. "What do you mean you're not going to get better?"

"It's true, old pal. It's quite final. But listen, today I'm not thinking about it. So let's not start."

I was a little sore at myself. We've all got to go, I thought. It's like waiting for an alarm to go off, when it's too dark to read the dial. Looking at Dan's great chest straining his policeman's suspenders, it was fairly unimaginable that anything predictable could turn him to dust. I was quite wrong about that too.

A solitary antelope buck stopped to look at us from a great distance. Dan put his hat on the barrels of his gun and decoyed the foolish animal to thirty yards before it snorted and ran off. We had sometimes found antelope blinds the Indians had built, usually not far from the eagle traps, clever things made by vital hands. There were old cartridge cases next to the spring, lying in the dirt, 45–70s; maybe a fight, maybe an old rancher hunting antelope with a cavalry rifle. Who knows. A trembling mirage appeared to the south, blue and banded with hills and distance. All around us the prairie creaked with life. I tried to picture the Indians, the soldiers. I kind of could. Were they gone or were they not?

"I don't know if I want to shoot a limit."

"Let's find them first," I said. I would have plenty of time to think about that remark later.

Dan thought and then said, "That's interesting. We'll find them and decide if we want to limit out or let it stand." The pointers got up, stretched their backs, glanced at us, wagged once, and lay down again next to the spring. I had gotten a queer feeling. Dan went quiet. He stared off. After a minute, a smile shot over his face. The dogs had been watching for that, and we were all on our feet and moving.

"This is it," Dan said, to the dogs or to me; I was never sure which. Betty and Sally cracked off, casting into the wind, Betty making the bigger race, Sally filling in with meticulous groundwork. I could sense Dan's pleasure in these fast and beautiful bracemates.

"When you hunt these girls," he said, "you've got to step up their rations with hamburger, eggs, bacon drippings—you know, mixed in with that kibble. On real hot days, you put electrolytes in their drinking water. Betty comes into heat in April and October; Sally, March and September. Sally runs a little fever with her heat and shouldn't be hunted in hot weather for the first week and a half. I always let them stay in the house. I put them in a roading harness by August first to get them in shape. They've both been roaded horseback."

I began to feel dazed and heavy. Maybe life wasn't something you lost at the end of a long fight. But I let myself off and thought, These things can go on and on.

Sally pitched over the top of a coulee. Betty went in and up the other side. There was a shadow that crossed the deep grass at the head of the draw. Sally locked up on point just at the rim, and Dan waved Betty in. She came in from the other side, hit the scent, sank into a running slink, and pointed.

Dan smiled at me and said, "Wish me luck." He closed his gun, walked over the rim, and sank from sight. I sat on the ground until I heard the report. After a bit the covey started to get up, eight dusky birds that went off on a climbing course. I whistled the dogs in and started for my truck.

South Kensington produces London's best evenings. English ladies appear from the Pakistani grocer heading for residential hotels and recently converted mews. Old church spires preside over the latest generation of buggy English youth trickling through the tolerant neighborhood. They are still outnumbered by the men in bowlers, but many of the latter are modern offshore phonies, completing the destruction of England.

In front of Blake's small hotel, Bobby Decatur, an American, thirty, helplessly exudes privilege in his tweed jacket, Levi's, and cowboy boots. He is watching a striking American girl named Marianne climb out of a limousine. He doesn't know her. The chauffeur cuts his eyes at Bobby. Bobby is steadfast in his examination of her legs. She stoops for her belongings.

Bobby Decatur says, "Need a hand?"

She walks right by him and pulls open the glass door.

Bobby says, "Whore."

"You wish," replies the girl. The door closes behind her, and her image shimmers off and evaporates in the glass.

At the desk a Dutch girl named Hildegarde, who wears smart designer clothes every day and who directs the sallow Cockney bellhop, gives Marianne the key and says, "That's your new room. Away from the noisy landing. A little nicer, that. Room Two-ten."

Bobby listens from inside the door. When Marianne disappears up the stairs, Bobby approaches Hildegarde, who says, "This one is not for you," in the voice of a procurer. The American does a burlesque Who-me? And Hildegarde adds, "She is visiting her fiancé. A nice Englishman."

So Bobby Decatur goes across the foyer and down the stairs into the stainless-steel decor of the lounge. Jack the bartender has a crinkled face and a Prince Valiant haircut. He reminds Bobby that he is cut off. Bobby states that he has a letter from his doctor attesting that an unfortunate side effect of his medication goes a long way toward explaining his erratic behavior. Jack says that we've all got one of those doctors.

"Anyway," says Bobby, "it's not for me. I'm sending a drink to a friend. My mother, actually." Bobby sends a boilermaker to room 210 with a note explaining that English fiancés are undesirable. He invites Marianne to Deadrock, Montana, and signs his name.

"Thanks a million, Jack. Love your haircut. Put that on my room."

Marianne and her fiancé are sitting in Scott's Restaurant, off Park Lane. The best of the John Bull atmosphere with professional men of seafood shucking oysters behind a zinc bar. Ma-

rianne is just luscious, while her friend seems to have been
hand-carved from slabs of cold salt pork.

He says, "You are heroic to have come. A little fish will
help with the lag. The wine will make you sleep. I have a
meeting with a distinguished do-wop band, after which I'm
yours. You do look sleepy."

"As of yet, Allen, the trip hasn't gotten to me."

"I think you are spectacular."

Through the reversed lettering of the glass front window,
Bobby Decatur is holding a sign that reads, THAT MAN IS A CUR.
Marianne sees it.

"Darling, are you dizzy?"

"No," she says, "but I must go to the ladies'. Back in a jiff."

Outside, Marianne says to Bobby, "Leave me alone, you
little shit. And I put that drink you sent in the toilet."

"The loo."

"What?"

"It's called the loo in England. Get with it."

"I'm going in."

At the table, the fiancé asks, "Better?" The record industry
has given him the remote gape of a rock star.

"Much."

"You look distressed."

"I'm being pestered."

"And by whom?"

"An evidently crazy young man."

"I'm going to stop him."

"Actually, he's back in New York. I'm afraid it's still on
my mind."

"Shaking his thing in doorways, I suppose."

"But he's half charming. Anyway, darling, he's thousands
of miles away. Not to bother."

"Half charming?"

□ □ □

Bobby is in his clean plain room at Blake's. There are many very old well-bound books. There are many fine engravings of hunting hawks. On its perch, weathering in front of an open window, is a hooded falcon. Bobby presses his fist forward, and the hawk steps up onto his wrist. He draws the hooded bird close to his face and whispers, "Hello, in there. I've met a girl."

Bobby buys a chicken at the Kensington grocer, a whole chicken. He descends to the underground and rides in silence, carrying the chicken in his lap. He heads for a tattoo parlor near Knightsbridge.

At the end of the day, Hildegarde, at the front desk in Blake's, hands Marianne a beautifully wrapped box. Marianne takes it to her room and removes her coat. She sits on the bed and opens the box. The chicken lies nestled in excelsior, its breast tattooed *Born to raise hell*.

Marianne smiles.

A middle-aged couple living on the first floor of Blake's idly dismembers the morning *Times* on their patio while eating breakfast. A dead mouse falls on the table. The gentleman lets his gaze travel upward to the falcon pacing nervously on the balcony above, fretting over its own lost breakfast.

At the front desk, Hildegarde says to Marianne, "Never mind the Portobello Road. It's all queers selling Marilyn Monroe pictures."

"I need a sweater and souvenir paperweights for my nieces."

"What was in it?"

"In what?"

"The box."

"A chicken."

"A chicken! I think that is the height of rudeness. In my country it is considered inappropriate to send a lady a chicken."

"It was delicious," lies Marianne defensively.

The manager is at Bobby's door. He's a Midlands fellow with surfacing blood vessels in the points of his cheeks.

"Mr. Decatur, we've had a complaint as to the bird. Mr. and Mrs. Tripp downstairs assert that it is dropping mice amid their breakfast." His right hand illustrates the downward progress of a mouse in air. "The bird," he adds.

"I have arranged to sell the bird to an Arab."

"Not because of this small complaint—"

"I'm returning to the United States of America. I've met a girl, and it is impractical to transport falcons on commercial aircraft."

"Actually, there's an Arab gentleman in the lobby just now, actually."

"It's our man. Send him whilst I dust the bird."

A short time later, a rather bouncy sheikh sits in Bobby's room, in a leather chair. His kaffiyeh is very well lighted by a standing lamp. He has the carriage of a lazy natural athlete.

"I feel you have overpriced the hawk, Bobby."

"Say, Sheikh, you need a prairie falcon. The American West, get it?"

"Five thousand is a joke."

"It's an Arab's job to pay too much."

"If I give this kind of money, I'm compromised each time I try to buy an American hawk."

"I know what you offered the Air Force Academy for the Arctic falcon."

"That's different. I was in Colorado. I was skiing. I was

167

tooted out. And it could have been taken as a political gesture. Exxon was on every slope."

"What kind of airplane do you have?"

"De Havilland with a custom galley. When it's on autopilot, the pilot cooks. What does that have to do with it?"

"A week with the plane and the hawk is a gift."

The sheikh unwinds his rig from about his ears as he thinks. It makes the sheikh's beard seem wrong.

"Bobby, it's a deal. You should have been a pimp."

"It's never too late."

In Blake's small dining room, Bobby and Marianne sit at separate tables, though tiny rippling energy waves connect them. Bobby sends Marianne a Shirley Temple. Marianne sends Bobby a Bionic Boy. These concoctions are like the filaments sent out by warring spiders.

Marianne calls out, "Thank you, it's fantastic! But don't drop by the table to discuss it!"

"Can I interest you in a martial-arts film festival?"

"Gosh, no."

Marianne gets up from her table and walks to Bobby's.

"Don't get up. Listen, you're terribly interesting. But I'm here to see my fiancé, and you're a vulgar little shit."

"I have a de Havilland and an MEA pilot who cooks."

"Right, and then I'm going back to the United States. It's silly, really it is, to spend your time on something that isn't happening. Isn't happening, got it?"

Bobby hears a knock on the door of his room. When he opens it, there is Marianne. He says, "Come in, come in." No surprise here. Atop her in no time.

"Got anything to read?"

"Sure do. A history of falconry in Persia do?"

"Just right," says Marianne. Bobby fishes the old volume off the shelf and hands it to her.

"I'm going to the country with my fiancé. I need something to read. Haven't got your bookplate in here, do you?"

"No, I don't."

"Good, thanks, 'bye."

Gone.

"You be sure and bring that book back. It's—it's—" Bobby goes to the empty falcon perch. "It's my book."

Bobby Decatur is all alone in an unsuccessful tearoom.

"A weekend can be a long time when you're missing someone. Darling, it was an eternity. I thought of you in the country with an Englishman the color of putty. And I ached. I really did."

A waiter peers at Bobby from the doorway.

The Silver Cloud cruises from Iver Heath. Do-wop millions, in relatively stable pounds, pay the freight.

"I don't think you ever took the trouble to get Mummy's point of view."

"Mummy has a problem," says Marianne to her fiancé.

"Which is?"

"She's an absolute pill."

"Oh, God."

"That's my point of view."

"See over there? Next to the Hogarth Laundry? That's where the engraver Hogarth lived."

"Got a plaque?"

"Yes, Marianne. The house is history, Marianne. Therefore the plaque."

"Then I want a plaque for us."

British Airways flashes in the window of the Silver Cloud.

"So, that's how it is."

At the desk in Blake's, Marianne tells Hildegarde she would like to leave the American a message.

"What did you do with that chicken?"

Marianne requests of the Dutch girl that she not be impertinent. They once were friends. Now Marianne stares at her and concludes: a real cluck. Hildegarde.

"I told you once, Hildegarde. I ate it."

One room of the British Museum contains a Norse ship whose swept dragon-shaped prow dominates the venerable space. Bobby and Marianne, together at last, are in its dusty shadow.

Bobby says, "Look at it, Marianne. I always come to see the Viking stuff. Can you imagine building a boat like that and then invading England, kicking their rotten little monasteries into the Atlantic?"

A glass case holds a Viking skull, splendid in a winged helmet. Bobby is in rapture.

"Now there's who I want to be."

A peregrine scatters larks in a vivid diorama.

"Falcons take splash baths in clear water about ten times a day. If they get mites and little parasites other birds take for granted, they lose their edge and can no longer win the game of survival. If they lose one percent of their pure efficiency in killing, they are the ones to die."

An illuminated Bible from the Middle Ages catches his eye for bright colors. Bobby is explaining everything.

"The only people in the world like Vikings and falcons are pimps. They prey on the world. Look at that God damned Bible. That's the book that put Joe Blow in the driver's seat. It's a regular operation manual."

"I want something to eat."

"A pimp doesn't care if he ever eats again."

"If we find the right restaurant we can make beautiful music together. *What do pimps have to do with it?*"

It was an awful restaurant. Both Bobby and Marianne ordered so as not to upset the waiter. Then the waiter was rude. But they were scared of him.

"How did you meet the Englishman?"

"He was in their trade commission. Now he's a music producer with a specialty in do-wop."

"What did you lobby for?"

"Meat byproducts."

"Women have the hearts of assassins."

"These big statements, Bobby! We've got some difficult eating ahead of us." The waiter brings their ghastly platters, gratuity in the price.

The rakish de Havilland jet has Arabic writing on the fuselage. Bobby leads Marianne aboard. All is luxury-thick aluminum.

"Marianne, meet Abdul. He bombed a kibbutz and can really cook." Abdul is the first pilot Marianne has seen in a fez. He has twinkling eyes.

The jet heads out over the Atlantic. The navigator serves drinks to Bobby and Marianne. They are keen on the upholstery. Later, Bobby attempts to seduce Marianne by putting his hand up her dress and fiddling awkwardly with her underthings as though he were trying to retrieve a letter through a mail slot. After a good deal of this, he spots America through the window. He also notices Abdul and the navigator watching to see if he's going to get his thing into Marianne.

When he closes the door to the cockpit, he says, "Watch where you're going or you'll ram America."

Then Bobby does something strange. He pulls a gun on Marianne and yells for her to undress. When she is naked she lies on the floor with her feet on either side of the aisle. Bobby

171

mounts her as the airplane sinks into the atmosphere of America. The wings make an eerie chiming as they angle toward the coast.

In the taxicab, New York goes unnoticed. Bobby and Marianne are discussing her rape.

Marianne says, "If it hadn't been for the peering Arabs, the airplane would have been a good place to make love."

"What about when I pulled the gun?"

"I thought it was pretentious."

At last they take a room at the Pierre. Though the room has a handsome view, they have thus far avoided looking at New York. Only after two orange juices have been delivered does Bobby go to the window.

"There are some very remarkable hawks that live on the tops of those buildings," he says, "and they bang into the shit-heel pigeons for dinner."

"I thought we were going to Deadrock, Montana. Even the cur took me to the country."

"To Mummy's place, so he could bop you in his old playroom."

"That's enough."

"Spreading yourself thin."

"Bobby, you're jealous. How very nice." Marianne beams without guile, two thousand miles from the chicken.

Then rather strangely, Bobby says, "I don't know why we came here."

"I don't either."

"I thought coming back to America would give us a sense of starting over."

"I don't want to start over. I want to have a nice time."

"We have to find a place to live, a place with the atmosphere of home. But before that, let's send out for a whore."

"For what?"

"Inspirational chats."

Marianne gazes at him with serene gray eyes.

"Let me ask you this, do you have a mother?"

"Yes, I do," says Bobby.

"And where does she live?"

"She recently moved to the Carlyle."

"From where?"

"Deadrock, Montana."

"Are we going to see her? Is that why we're here?"

"Yes, one reason."

"Is it to get money?"

"There is that."

At the Oyster Bar in Grand Central Station, Bobby says, "That is it, the best oyster stew in America. Little wonder Lillian Hellman chose this for the site of her soiree. Did she have it at Twenty-one? No, she had it at the Oyster Bar because she knew the city and she knew her oysters."

"Bobby?"

"What?"

"May we order?"

After Bobby has gone on and on about hookers and they are now in a corridor of the Carlyle Hotel, Marianne states the following in no uncertain terms:

"What you would do with a hooker is your own problem. I have no interest in hookers. And what does that have to do with your mother? Let's see her first, and please may we get off the subject of hookers. I am increasingly suspicious that you are treating me like one."

The door swings open and there stands Emily Decatur, Bobby's mother. She has neatly arrayed silver hair and wears a Dale Evans cowgirl suit.

She says, "Howdy, Bob. And who might this be?"

"Marianne, a sport from Duluth. Mother is a cowgirl from New York, Deadrock, and Santa Barbara."

"Come in. How do you do. Come right in."

Amid the French walnut furniture are barbed-wire collections, western bronzes, and mounted arrowhead collections. Leaning against a fine old armoire are a couple of wagon wheels.

"How broke are you, Bob?"

"Fairly broke. It wouldn't be so bad but I have plans."

"So, something new."

"It's been on the back burner," says Bobby. "But I'd be in motion, I think, if I had the wherewithal."

"This is where the rich old broad comes in," says Emily Decatur to Marianne, a speech which, in the atmosphere Bobby has tried to induce, seems brightly candid.

"I'm afraid it is," says Bobby, preserving sincerity.

"Would the Deadrock ranch be a help?"

"Would I have to run it?"

"It's been leased out for twenty years. You'd need to supply an address, though, if you wanted the checks to come to you. Are you up to that?"

"Yes, that would be very nice."

"Then it's yours," says Emily Decatur. "Would you like an aerial photograph of it?"

"Not really."

"Are you sure? You can see the little homestead, and tiny figures of cows and horses."

"Thanks, but I don't really want it."

"Okay, it's a deal then," says Emily Decatur, pumping her son's hand.

"That's quite a gesture, Ma. Say, thanks for the nice ranch."

"The West is where it all begins."

"I think so."

"You're free, Bob."

"That's what the West is for, Ma, to make men free."

"Now what're you going to do?"

"I'm going to San Francisco to become a pimp."

Bobby is staring from the window while Marianne does her makeup at a little desk. Bobby opens the door to permit a room-service waiter to push a linen-covered cart in and set up a table.

"How many places shall I set, sir?"

"Three, and keep the entrees in the warmer, as we are not yet ready to dine."

The waiter sets out melons, cheese, and red and white wines while Bobby signs the check. He wishes the waiter a spirited *"Andale, muchacho!"* as he goes.

"Hungry, darling?"

"Famished, but I want to get my eyes on first."

Marianne has made herself up vividly, like a courtesan. A knock.

Bobby admits Adrienne, a brown-eyed handsome young lady.

"Just right," Bobby cries. "Oh, goody."

"Hello, I'm Adrienne."

"And this is Marianne. I'm Bobby Decatur. I've taken the liberty of ordering you some lovely noisettes of lamb. Marianne is having coquilles Saint-Jacques and I—I'm having a cheeseburger, and I really don't want a cheeseburger but I want to soak in the tub and watch you two dine and chat. I think the cheeseburger will be a little handier. The prospects of the entree floating between one's knees will be eliminated."

Adrienne says, "Here's one with his mind in the gutter."

"I'm no real animal," Bobby objects, as he stacks hundreds on the table. "That should cover the eventualities."

Soon Bobby floats in the tub, idly nipping at the cheeseburger, spurting soap from his free hand, and gleefully peering out through the bathroom door.

"Aw, come on in!"

"No!"

"Adrienne has to!"

"You said we were partners!" retorts Marianne strangely.

At the table, Adrienne says, "He must look like a prune by now. Hey, what do you guys want from me?"

"I think he's looking for a life story."

"No chance."

Bobby asks Adrienne to undress and bring him some french fries. Even naked, Adrienne seems so different that the french fries acquire the status of clothes. At any rate, they soon make a tiny log jam in the tub. Bobby climbs out, scrutinizes Adrienne, touches a thing or two, and wraps himself in a towel. When they come out of the bathroom, Marianne is unclothed.

"Want to see mine?" she asks. "Bobby, you and Adrienne should go to bed together."

"All it takes is money," says Adrienne. Bobby is mortified by this burst of actuality. He commands Marianne to dress.

"Adrienne, look! His face is red!"

"I thought this was his idea."

"He's full of ideas. It's quite lovable. He has a big inheritance, and all he wants is to be a pimp."

"Oh, for God's sake! I'm leaving," says Adrienne.

At the door, Bobby and Marianne call out good night to Adrienne. Then, mute, they stare at one another.

"It wasn't my idea."

"I didn't say it was a bad idea."

"At least it didn't cost anything."

Bobby says, "I felt that girl was on the cynical side."

"Nobody knew what you had in mind."

"No, no, no. That's not it. What I was feeling was that you two felt I knew but that I had lost my nerve."

"You had."

When Bobby bursts into the hallway, he says, "We'll see about this!" He goes off in his bathrobe.

Marianne follows him to the elevators. A bellhop is standing there, and Bobby says to him, "I want a whore!"

"This isn't that kind of hotel, sir."

"It isn't? I just sent one off. Now I want another."

"No."

"What?"

"No."

In the lobby, Bobby pushes through clients of the hotel to the front desk. The clerk, in uniform, has seen all of this he wants to.

"I'm in Four-eighteen and I want a whore."

"That's out of the question."

"Gimme that phone. This hotel needs hookers. Do you hear me?"

"Four-eighteen? You have thirty minutes to vacate Four-eighteen or I'll see to it that New York's finest do it for you."

Bobby's draining face seems to be superimposed on those of the outraged guests. Marianne has subtly blended in among them.

She asks, "Who is that young man?"

Soon Marianne sits atop the luggage outside. Bobby comes out of a phone booth. His spirits are a little droopy.

"Can't get a room anywhere. We're leaving this terrible city where even the smallest civilities are nonexistent."

Bobby and Marianne sit under the vague circles of the reading lights. Rows of sleeping hands, resting upon armrests, stretch down the aisles toward the captain and crew, who cautiously adjust the 747's triggers for the Pacific.

"When I get tired," Bobby says, "I get scared."

"I do too. I think about the plane falling."

"I think we're very tired. I'm scared and I don't even know what of."

"Don't say that," says Marianne. "I'm completely terrified."

"What do you think it is?"

"San Francisco. I think something is waiting for us in San Francisco. And I don't know what it is."

Bobby imagines fog; the airplane penetrates a low ceiling to an eerie groundscape. "We're just tired," he says.

"That's not the whole story. The whole story is, the attraction is getting too—I don't know—too something."

Bobby says, "And pretty soon the ghosts of our past will emerge."

"How terrifying. How foul."

"We have to wipe it all out before it kills us."

By Nebraska, Marianne is asleep. Bobby has a reptilian restlessness the magazine rack can't sop up. He begins to move about the aisles, staring hard at the sleeping faces, avoiding those stunned by air travel, until he catches the eye of a traveler, a man in his thirties who is wide awake.

"How you doing?"

"Fine. Kind of a long deal at night, isn't it?"

"Sure is. Can I sit down?"

"Do, go right ahead."

"How come you're going to San Francisco?"

"I'm a maritime lawyer there."

"Married?" Bobby asks. He doesn't seem impertinent.

"Not yet."

"I'm looking for a kind of nice hotel. Something right in the middle of things."

"Stay at the Saint Francis. It's on Union Square. Couldn't be handier. You on business?"

"I just got out of one."

"Which was?"

"Hawk sales," says Bobby. The traveler doesn't show his bafflement.

"Now what're you going to do?"

"Kind of an escort service," says Bobby.

"How do you mean?"

"Arranging for girls."

"I see."

"Does that offend the heck out of your sensibilities?"

The traveler goes ha-ha-ha and says, "No, I just wish you had one with you."

Pause. "I do."

"Oh, God."

"You want her?"

"I don't see how."

"Let her figure it out. Hey! That's what they're for."

"What's it cost?"

"You be the judge. Seat Twelve-A. Wake her and tell her the deal is history. I'll keep your place until you get back."

The traveler rests his head in deep thought and then says, "Okay."

The traveler gently awakens the beautiful sleeping Marianne.

"I'm Jonathan."

"Hello."

"I've been speaking to your gentleman friend."

"And?"

"He said to tell you that we've come to an arrangement. May I sit down?"

Utah.

Jonathan sits and kisses Marianne full on the lips. She neither yields nor pulls away. He slides his hand up her dress.

"May I ask you what you think you're doing?"

"I should like to interest you . . . in love."

"Do you do this with all the passengers?"

"I just thought—I—"

"I know, Bobby told you he was a pimp. It's his way of passing the evening."

"I'm very sorry," says the traveler, rising. "But I must tell you, you left it a little ambiguous yourself."

"Please go back to your seat."

Bobby sits alone, his head against the rest, tilted back, in intense thought. He thinks he can make out the lights of Salt Lake City, but his view is abruptly interrupted by a sharp, open-handed slap across his face.

"May I have my seat?" the maritime lawyer inquires.

"Of course."

Not till the Ramada limo service does Marianne make mention of the odd event on the 747. She says, measuring her words, "Next time you do that, I'm going to go for it. So think about that."

"I'm going to be decent or know the reason why. My ears are ringing." Earnestness floods Bobby's face. He could cry.

"Like how?"

"I'm going to find us a good little house with a garden and a view of the sea. I'll get you books on Jane Austen and, for me, Ernest Hemingway. We will make war on meat by-products by elevating our minds. There will be days when we view paintings or relax at the Palace of the Legion of Honor."

A woman realtor named Jane Adams, who seems distinctly San Franciscan, shows them a hidden gem with a sea view above the Presidio. The city cascades at the feet of Bobby and Marianne. Jane Adams notes that it's a little bit of heaven for a young couple. Bobby gapes at her ass.

"We'll take it. We've got a couple of books to read and no telephone. Plus, we're looking for a small business together, something with no overhead."

Jane Adams laughs, directing her face across the city to the high seas.

"What are you laughing at?"

"I just had a silly thought. I really can't repeat it."

At first, Bobby and Marianne love their little house, with its latticed understory and the gleaming bladderworts of its small garden. There are absolutely no fleas in the carpet, and the front window is free of decals that would violate the view of the Pacific.

In the morning, pretty, foggy light reveals Marianne carrying coffee and croissants up the wooden stairs; then, side by side in the bed, the two agree not to turn on the "Today" show.

"I can smell the ocean in the curtains," says Marianne.

"That Barbara Walters is a real tire biter," says Bobby. "Is she on that show?"

"Your bathrobe makes me laugh."

"This marmalade was a good year."

"I think so."

"I want a book on the Tong wars. Those old Tongs had this town in knots. Underground tunnels, opium, captive girls."

"Let's go to Golden Gate Park today."

Really, they should never have gone to Golden Gate Park.

When they arrive at the casting pools, Bobby gazes at the well-dressed anglers with a certain terror.

"I would like you to note," he says, "that there are no fish in those waters."

"Those men are having a good time."

"Oh, great."

"It's not symbolic, Bobby."

When they get to the buffalo paddock and view the great mementos grazing in the coastal fog, Bobby says, "There you have it. The American West. I feel weak all over."

Bobby seems serious. He demands they go to a drugstore. "I don't feel so well." They buy a thermometer and take his temperature out on the sidewalk: normal. He announces that his hematocrit is out of whack and that he must be losing blood.

"I absolutely know that the ratio of red blood cells to plasma is way off. I felt it the minute I spotted those buffalo."

After the blood test, Bobby insists on the upper and lower GI series. The radiologist mans the machine in his lead apron while Bobby gulps barium. The radiologist slams plates in and out of the machine. Bobby feels at death's door in his odd gown.

At length, the doctor says, "Your blood's fine. Your mucosa patterns are exquisite. You're fine. Good-bye."

In the waiting room Bobby tells Marianne, "I've had a very close call. I'd like a nickel for every farewell speech I've composed. My life passed before my eyes, and I concluded, as anyone would, that there was not a minute to be lost. Let's hit the streets." Bobby takes Marianne down Maiden Lane and shows her Frank Lloyd Wright's initials on a red tile. Then he buys her a pair of silver pumps with bright macaws on their sides. Marianne stretches her pretty legs to smile at her shoes. In Joseph Magnin, Bobby seems hypnotized as Marianne tries on silk dresses. His heart is racing.

They stop at a park bench on Union Square with delicatessen sandwiches and a bottle of red wine or, rather, Pagan Pink. They pass the bottle back and forth as though they were hunkered down in some railroad yard.

Marianne says, "I was engaged twice and ducked out both times. I've been worried about life passing me by. I thought if I got married, that would happen, and I would disappear without a trace."

"I felt that when I saw those buffalo."

"In college I saw that if I improved my mind, I would always be broke. Then came meat byproducts."

"Now what?"

"Chance. And you, I guess."

At the dinner table, Marianne is dressed in her new clothes, her eyes and lips darkened savagely. She wears the silver shoes. The two have sent out for veal piccata. Neither has eaten yet. It's a matter of who goes for his gun first. Thin green candles burn, and the table is walnut. Bobby wears his Blake's Hotel clothes: Levi's, cowboy boots, chambray shirt, and a bottle-green velvet jacket.

"Let's hit it."

Despite the yearly deterioration of what used to be known as the passing scene into the current smarmy flux, Enrico's Sidewalk Café remains a grand spot to view it, whatever it is. There are those who would argue that this is on the order of a front-row seat at a nose-picking contest. But Enrico's customers don't feel that way. In any case, Bobby and Marianne sit at one of the sidewalk tables, demand tall, frosty drinks, and join the others on the lookout. Marianne's eyes fall naturally on a prosperous man in his forties, leaning on one hand and punching away at a calculator with his other.

Bobby would like to meet an astronaut. Marianne loves the breeze through her clothes. She has no interest in the kind of people who would leave a golf putter on the moon. Moreover, they would probably have to go elsewhere to meet astronauts. "Ever since you traded the bird to that Arab, we've been on the move."

A prostitute wanders across the front of the café, her legs slightly in front of her. She glances at the man with the calculator. Bobby watches, then flags down the bartender. He orders second drinks for himself and Marianne, then addresses the bartender.

"Say, is that young lady—is she in the life?"

"You'll have to ask her." The bartender grins and leaves for the drinks, ignoring thirty imploring hands.

"Marianne, excuse me a sec."

Marianne watches Bobby lope toward the prostitute. When he comes back, she wants to know what he said to her.

"Just got her name."

"And?"

"Some idea of prices. I had to tell her, you know, that I was interested. Her name is Donna. Anyway, she said a hundred. You're way prettier than she is."

"Thank you," says Marianne.

"Now what I'm thinking is, that guy over there with the calculator."

Slowly and imperturbably, Marianne gazes at the man. She looks back at Bobby a moment and gets up.

"I'll see you at home."

Marianne starts off bravely in her silver shoes. From either end of the cafe, Bobby and the prostitute Donna watch Marianne sit down with the man, who smiles and puts the calculator in his pocket. Marianne sips his drink.

Suddenly, down Broadway, with Stetson hats and cameras, comes a mob of Japanese tourists. Bobby, whose heart is already pounding, panics as they flood the area between him and

Marianne. He jumps up in complete fear and begins pushing through them. When he gets to the other side, Marianne and the man with the calculator are gone. He goes back to his table.

"Hey."

Dazed, Bobby looks up. It's Donna.

"What?"

"You get a price out of me, then send your trick to the guy. I don't think that's nice, 'n' that. Can I sit down?"

"Yuh."

"How many ladies you got?"

"Just one."

"What're you so depressed about?"

"Drinking these things in the sun."

"I mean, your hands are shaking."

"I've got Parkinson's disease."

"You want to stop by my place? You look like you could use a pick-me-up."

"Yeah, all right."

They go up Broadway, past the Hotel Du Midi, the Basque restaurant, past the Chinese novelty shops, more or less in silence as Bobby continues to bear his stricken look; then up an alley to a stairway, a catwalk, and a door.

They enter a small neat flat with gridded outside light coming in from above, some books, and, sitting in a Mexican goatskin sling chair, a very bad-looking man named Chino, whose name, a nickname, comes from a correctional facility in southern California. His real name is Donald Arthur Jones. He waves with professional indolence but still manages to look dangerous. He says, "Hey, Donna. Look, am I in the way? Just say so. Who's our friend?"

"I don't know, baby. But you assured me Enrico's was your spot. And this guy and his whore run off a customer on me about five minutes ago, which embarrasses me on your behalf."

"Gimme your name."

"Bobby Decatur."

"Donna, get Bobby the pictures."

Donna takes a stack of Polaroids off the bookshelf and sets them on the table.

"C'mere, Bobby," says Chino. "C'mere and sit next to me." Bobby does; it looks like a piano duet. Bobby looks through a stack of pictures of a man who has been maimed with a knife. Chino begins to speak in a comically deep voice.

"This man took a girl to Enrico's. This girl was in the life. They turned a few dollars. This is what he got."

"Is he dead?"

"In some ways. Now this was done with a Buck folding knife, which is very nice for an off-the-shelf knife. It's stainless steel, and though it's difficult to sharpen, it will hold an edge indefinitely. Lately, I have my knives custom-made for me in Lawndale, California, by a man who is a craftsman, perhaps even an artist. What is the catch? A two-year waiting list. He's the only man in the world who can make me wait. So for a while I made do with the off-the-shelf folding knife like some nimrod, Bobby. Donna, show Bobby the Lawndale master-piece."

Donna fetches an ivory-handled dagger.

"Bobby, with one motion I could throw your insides halfway up Russian Hill. So why don't you and Mrs. Scumbag find some fast-food place that would form a more suitable background for your talent and her looks."

"I saved the best part," says Donna. "The john she picked up was a cop." This, thinks Bobby, has become extremely sordid.

All the way to jail, Bobby says, "Oh, God, God, God. Oh, God." But gradually he draws himself together and does the right thing under the circumstances by posting a bond. Once they've gotten into a cab, Bobby attempts to alleviate the chill between himself and Marianne.

"I want to go to the Imperial Palace," he says. "Or any restaurant with integrity and a serious kitchen. I don't want some fluorescent-lit noodle pavilion. I want a fine old Chinese restaurant like the Imperial Palace."

"You God damned son of a bitch."

"Yes. That's what I thought you were thinking."

But they go anyway and fit themselves into the darkness of the restaurant among the silk paintings, cloisonné, and velvet panels. There are long-stemmed roses on the table. Bobby raises his drink and bravely pronounces the following:

"At least you didn't have to go through with it."

"Are you joking? The cop had me before the arrest. I thought I was making us money. I thought it was what we wanted."

The waiter arrives.

"Oh, please no, Marianne. My God, I—let me order for both of us. Waiter! We shall each have Eight Precious soup. I want squab Macao, and my wife will have Five Willows rock cod with loquats, kumquats, and sweet pickles."

The waiter departs. Bobby says, "I'm just stricken. I'm heartbroken."

"I thought this was your fantasy, asshole! And I'm not your wife."

"Oh, right, hang that one on me."

"Since we met, I broke up with my fiancé, I left a good job, I was raped in an Arab jet, jailed, and taken to a Chinese restaurant."

Silence. What a dreadful summation, thinks Bobby.

"Is that all you have to say for our romance?"

"Bobby, that is what has happened!"

In the dark hole of their bedroom, Bobby and Marianne watch television.

Bobby says, "When I'm desperate, I love Johnny Carson."

Marianne says, "When I'm desperate, I love Walter Cronkite. Besides, Johnny Carson is supposed to have a monster coke habit."

"Let's plant a garden tomorrow."

By midmorning, Bobby has spaded a loamy spot in the backyard. Marianne cultivates on her hands and knees. Bobby is a handsome zombie.

"If we could just make one thing grow," Bobby says. "Well, it would make a difference."

"What kind of seeds did you buy?"

Bobby fishes the packets from his shirt pocket. "Radishes, peonies, watermelon, and what's this? Some kind of banana or something."

"Well, you can count on the radishes. Give me those."

"You can't have a garden with just radishes."

"What's the matter with you, Bobby? That's nothing to get upset about. Let me see these. That's summer squash, Bobby, that's not a banana. Can't you see that?"

"I don't care."

"Don't you want to have a garden?"

Bobby and Marianne are lucky enough to join the happy browsers at Ghirardelli Square, a place well known for the character of its great chocolate candies, which make one's fillings ring like a carillon. Bobby's usual propensity not to be normal seems far away today, and he holds Marianne's hand in blind euphoria, driving not a few walkers from the crowded sidewalk. It has come time for him to explain it all to Marianne.

"This is one of those places where people pretend that there is no unhappiness. There can be unhappiness at Fisherman's Wharf but not at Ghirardelli Square. At Fisherman's Wharf, though you may bump into Joe DiMaggio, that still does not prevent you from toppling into the sea. But here you will never meet anyone bad or have anything happen to you."

"There is no unhappiness at Neiman-Marcus," Marianne replies. "Many cities have little areas of no unhappiness. Even the Russians are beginning to build them."

"Marianne, I'm lucky to have such a smart girl."

By the time they get home again, Marianne is filled with a cheerful interest in making something of Bobby's banana garden, while clouds have once more settled on Bobby's face. In fact, he's soon indoors unwrapping his Smith and Wesson from an oily rag on the walnut surface of the dining-room table. He loads every chamber with the gleaming copper-and-lead bullets, snaps the cylinder back, and puts the gun in his pocket.

"Babe, I'm going to the store. Back in an hour."

Bobby scrutinizes the customers at Enrico's until he finds the hooker Donna. He speaks affably to her, even though she greets him as "the new kid in town."

"Hey," he says. "I guess my girl and me stepped all over everybody's toes. Which we didn't mean to do. I just wanted to say I sure was sorry. So, this is me saying sure am sorry."

"That's all right. Chino came down pretty hard on you."

"Yeah, he did. But he was right. I was gonna stop by and tell him he was right."

"Well, he's there."

"Should I just fall by?"

"Let me tell him you're coming."

Bobby takes this opportunity to leave enough money at the bar to keep Donna drinking until he sees her again. Donna returns from the pay phone. "I told him how you were feeling. He said stop on by. Chino said he don't hold no grudges if you don't. But I should warn you: he's after your lady."

Bobby heads up the familiar alley, climbs the fire escape, and on the landing is greeted by a really charming Chino, the former Donald Arthur Jones.

He says, "I understand that you are here to prove that you are a gentleman."

"I like revisiting the scene of the crime."

"Crime?" Chino grins. "What crime?"

Bobby gazes around the room. "The crime against taste in this creephole you call home. What do you want with those plaster Buddhas? Are you a Buddhist? And that beanbag chair? You make enough money. Is your crud taste necessary?"

Chino stares serenely at Bobby. After a moment, he asks, "Where is the gun?"

"How come lowlifes have always got hippie books on their bookshelf? What's this, *Watership Down? The Hobbit?* What a soft heart you must have. Let's have something to eat."

In the kitchen, Bobby takes a plate down from the cabinet and gets some silverware out of a drawer. He sets a place. He goes to the refrigerator and takes out a container.

"Mind if I take some of this organic yogurt?"

"Nope."

"I think it's wonderful you should be having all these wonderful things. They're so good for your karma. What do you do, sit down with the *Mother Earth News,* eat some yogurt, and then go knife somebody?"

"Not quite."

"Join me," Bobby orders. He seems possessed. He's thinking of killing Chino, but he's modulated that to possession. Chino sits.

"Where are those pictures you showed me the other day?"

"Under the bookend."

Bobby wanders absently into the other room. He doesn't remember the bookend. Chino gets up and quietly begins to follow him. He picks up Bobby's dinner knife. As he clears the corner, Bobby swings the short heavy revolver into his face. Chino drops the silverware and totters around like an old man, holding his face and cooing. Bobby strolls back with the pictures and gestures for Chino to sit down. He sits.

"This is dinner. This is what you're gonna eat, Chino."

"I can't eat those. I can't eat Polaroids. They've got chemicals on them."

"You have to eat them. If you don't, I can't answer for my actions. You can put any seasoning on them you like." Bobby throws the ghastly pictures on Chino's plate, one by one.

"What's this one?"

"My kid. Name of Jesse."

"How old is he?"

"Ten."

"He looks about three in this picture. You shouldn't have this picture in here. Who's his mother?"

"Used to be one of my girls," says Chino gloomily.

"You don't have to eat those pictures."

Bobby wanders disconsolately out the door. The curtain is falling.

"See you."

" 'Bye."

Donna's features have grown vaguer since Bobby left. He sits down next to her. She says, "I've been cocktailing since you left. Thanks for the drinks."

"I feel the best thing would be for you to come back to my place."

"What'd you say to Chino?"

"Not that much."

"Did you hit him?"

"Once I had to."

"You hit him . . . ?"

"Had to."

"I'll come with you. Will I be able to work?"

"That's the whole idea."

"Here's the thing. You've made it so I have to hide out, and, like, I've had to hide before. But you're not necessarily my next guy."

"How many of you are there?"

"Four."

"Names?"

"Jan, Marielle, and La Costa. And Donna."

"All Caucasian?"

"La Costa is Negro. We never see Marielle. She went to college. She has her own clients. She buys municipal bonds."

"Is this all you guys do?"

"Jan dances. What about your lady?"

"I'm in love with her. I could marry her. It could happen. She's Caucasian."

"All the pimps fall in love with La Costa. If you see Chino again, it will be because of La Costa."

Before they ever get inside the door, Bobby wants to know how Donna likes the view. She says, "It's great." Bobby asks her if she remembers tricking him into going to Chino's the first time.

"Yes. . . ."

Bobby slams her across the face. She takes two staggering

steps with her arms hanging. "That was the last mistake you're allowed."

Marianne opens the door in time to glimpse the blow. Bobby is a bit breathless from the adrenaline; it was like real exposure in rock climbing. Marianne asks what's going on.

Bobby says, "I was just explaining to Donna that the fastest way to get a low red-cell count is to have someone cut your throat." He feels the gravity on his noggin.

But Donna is the first to go into the house, introducing herself to Marianne as she passes. When they follow her in, Marianne says, to improve the situation, "I'm afraid Bobby sees himself as dangerous."

"I'm afraid of what else he sees," says Donna.

"Have you eaten?"

"Not today. I sat around Enrico's, and I guess I drank too much. Bunch of mixed drinks."

In the kitchen, Marianne begins to reheat some homemade lentil soup for Donna, who is applying cleansing cream under her eyes, reverting to the plain midwestern girl she is. The day is done. Soon she is tucked in, in the spare bedroom. Bobby puts cheese melba toast and a glass of wine next to her bed. He works the tiny concerns to the point of dowdiness.

"You might get an appetite during the night. Tomorrow, we get your clothes."

"Thank you."

"And maybe we can ring up the other girls for a drink in the evening."

"Maybe," says Donna, eyeing his lips for slobber. No sign.

"Y'know what I mean."

"I know."

Upstairs, while Marianne lies in bed reading, Bobby stretches out on the floor and sketches the floor plan of the house on a large sheet of butcher paper. Marianne thinks for a moment; then it dawns on her. "If you're planning on turning this into a whorehouse, count me out. I don't see that as an intelligent atmosphere."

"What else could you do?" asks Bobby maladroitly.

"I could go back to work! Working in a whorehouse is not the only option I have! I never had such a discussion until I met you!"

"You were the one who took on that cop with such alacrity."

"Not alacrity, you bastard, I was fool enough to indulge myself in your wishful thinking."

"Which I see you now resent."

"You bet your life! And especially since you don't seem to have any conviction about it yourself. Listen to me, Bobby, I am reading a nice book by Jane Austen, and tonight I have no further desire to discuss whorehouses. Go talk to the whore downstairs, if you can't stand the pressure. I'm reading my book."

"I might."

I am on probation for soliciting. One slip and I will be jailed or assigned to community service. I prefer Jane Austen."

"I'm going downstairs to talk to Donna."

Bobby's bathrobe trails behind him as he descends. Bobby opens the spare room. It is empty. The drawers on the first floor are all pulled out. Marianne's purse is upended, looted. He turns his wallet inside out in futile hope. When he treads upstairs and back into the bedroom, Marianne inquires, without looking up from her book, "We been robbed?"

"Yup."

"Did she eat the little snacks you left by her little table?"

"I guess there wasn't time."

Bobby goes to bed, outfitted in disappointment. Yet once the lights are off, he falls into a deep sleep, dreaming of ambulance service in the Ardennes. Then he wakes up and snaps the light. Marianne is already awake, lost, her eyes going nowhere.

"Darling?"

"What, baby?"

"Have you had thousands of lovers?" he asks.

"Oh, babe."

"Tell me."

"No," she says.

"How many?"

"I don't know, darling."

"You don't even know how many?"

"I didn't count."

"Count. You mean it would be necessary to start counting?"

"Oh, Bobby, can't we just sleep?"

"I have to get this off my chest."

"Why do you have to?"

"I can't sleep," says Bobby. "Under fifty?"

"I think so."

"But close."

"Bobby, I don't know! My God, we don't even make love ourselves lately!"

"What a heartache I've got."

"I'm starting to get mad!"

"Don't get mad at me. My heart is aching, God damn it!"

"If you've got such a heartache, why are you trying to turn me into a hooker?"

"To wipe those aches away!"

"Well, let me tell you right now, I'm not about to reconstruct my past for you. So you can quit worrying about that one."

"Yeah, but you had one."

"So did you."

"It's not the same."

"Yes, it is."

"Did you sleep with that English rotter?"

"Obviously yes."

"I'll bet he was a bum lay."

"You'll never know."

"I can guess."

"Let's put it this way," says Marianne measuredly. "He beat the hell out of that plainclothesman."

"Don't keep running my face in that one!"

"Bobby, honey, you'd better figure out what you're up to. I mean, this is all very adventurous, but if you can't handle it, you better think of something you can."

"Is that some kind of attack on my nerve?" Bobby says sharply. Who is this dumb bunny trying to put on the spot?

Marianne has no trouble finding Donna at her predictable table the next day. The same bartender is in the corner like a heron spotting minnows.

"May we have our belongings back?"

"I don't know."

"That wasn't very nice."

"I'm not very nice. Blah, blah, blah."

"That's right," says Marianne. "You're a useless girl. And your fingerprints are on everything. I'm going from here to the police unless we can have our things back."

"Better have your boyfriend go. You've got a record."

"That's fine. Is that how you would prefer it?"

"I'll tell you something better. All your stuff is up to Chino's place, 'n' that. Your boyfriend went up and hassled my guy, and it was a question of my getting back in the first place. I'm not interested in being a house pet with a view of the ocean.

Part two, I love my guy. Can you follow that? If you want your stuff, go get it."

"Thank you very much, I will."

It must be that Chino can feel the vibration of someone on the fire escape because once more he is smiling on the landing, this time at brave Marianne, who seems primly ascending, like someone distributing leaflets for Jehovah's Witnesses.

"Good morning," she says. "I've come to see about my things."

Chino holds the door for her. Still sleepy, he looks more like Donald Arthur Jones; "Chino" is for as the day goes on. But it does seem the latter is coming on rather rapidly.

"Oh, yeah," he says. "The odds and ends Donna lifted. The money is in my bank and the credit cards are back in circulation."

"Well," Marianne says, feeling very much as though she were at the World Trade Center, "start thinking about how you're going to get them for me."

"Why?" Chino is narrowing down.

"Because we need them."

"Who? You and what's his name, Errol Flynn? Errol Flynn needs them. You don't."

"What's that mean?"

"That means you're not going anywhere. Errol Flynn is going to have to do his own cooking and washing until he can find some more live-in help. His old lady just found a new job."

"I'm looking for a girl named Donna. You remember, a tall brunette who sits at that table, that one there, next to the sidewalk?"

"I don't know her," says the bartender.

"Come on, she sits right there! I left a hundred bucks with you to cover her drinks."

"I don't remember that either."

"She's here every day!"

"Lower your voice or I'll have you bounced."

"I . . . I'm sorry. I have a job to do. I want to clean up this neighborhood. I could've used your help."

"Sorry."

"If it turns out I needed your help bad, I'm coming back to see you." Bobby's got his hand on the gun, and he'd like to shoot this fucker's lights out.

"Whatever blows your dress up," says the unflappable bartender as he swishes mai tai glasses in the suds.

Bobby stands on Chino's landing with his ear to the door. He can hear incoherent murmuring from within. He's got the gun in front of him and he's turning the knob as slowly as he can. The latch clicks and the door is free. Bobby kicks it wide open, jumping inside with the gun held two-handed, straight in front of him.

Three Chinese house painters babble in abject terror in the completely bare flat. Bobby gapes at the emptiness as he backs out amid the oriental cacophony.

"I'm sorry, I'm sorry, I'm terribly sorry. . . ."

"So sorry," they echo, nervously trying to get with it.

In a regally anonymous condominium, high in the middle of the city, each of whose windows gives onto a merciless view of the ocean and the far bridges of the bay, the silent corridors reach past the sealed doors like a nervous system. A door opens; a well-dressed man backs into the corridor trailing a woman's arm. It drops away and swings back into the doorway. He says thank you and goes. The girl is not Marianne; she is on the couch beyond in a nightgown. But the door closes.

□ □ □

At the Garden Court the next day, under the splendid green-house roof, Chino is having lunch with Marianne, whose terror and beautiful clothes have made her ravishing, beautiful. Chino is attempting a vain, somehow intimate speech to her. He seems to think only of Marianne.

"My job is to provide the illicit. Is that not so? In recent years I am up against hippies, sluts, and, worst of all, experimenters. And many of our country's people have become queer. What can I offer a successful man besides mere convenience? I am not McDonald's! I wish to be something more than a drive-up window. My clients are not . . . swingers! My clients are powerful, friends of the system. On the level of pure merchandise, they are happy with what I give and they . . . remunerate me so I can go on as a well-paid, quietly efficient person of crime. But . . . I think now I have something for the discerning, something which is not now easily obtained, not without crazy and needless risk. My clients have families and concerns; they need to express themselves."

"What is it you can offer them?" Marianne asks, in terror of this knife-wielding animal playing the gent at the table.

"I can offer them an unwilling lady, an intelligent woman who hates everything that is happening to her."

"But what if I learn to like it?" Marianne asks him desperately. Learning to like it is the only card she holds.

"Then you are just another one of the girls. You become commonplace."

"To whom?" A disappearing pulse of courage.

"To me, to yourself. What's the difference?"

Jane Adams, the lady realtor, a woman of energy and brains, is on the porch of Bobby's Presidio Heights house running down a rumor. Jane hates this. She wanted to make a living and this is it. The porch is covered with glass from a broken bottle that has been thrown from inside. Jane states as she enters, "Why not say it? I've had complaints."

The place is a mess, with half-finished meals and newspapers slung over the furniture.

"This certainly proves the value of a damage deposit," says Jane, hating the position she's in, this real-estate sham. Every time she has said "ranchette," "bungalow," "younger couple," "handyman's dream," has been, she now feels, a black mark on her soul. But Bobby's hauteur helps her through the moment.

"I couldn't agree more," he says jauntily.

"I'm thinking in terms of eviction."

"You'll need a hot lawyer."

"I'll get one. I rather thought your friend would be tidier."

"She's been kidnapped. Tough to be tidy, under the circumstances."

It's very quiet.

"Have you reported this to the police?"

"On, yes, first thing."

"And what happened?"

"They said she had merely left. She had a record, which they said indicated that she had simply moved on."

"A record for what?"

"Prostitution."

"Well, I would never have guessed that!"

"Please don't evict me. I'll get a maid."

"You look like you could cry."

"Can I touch you?" Bobby asks.

"We shook hands once," she said.

"Can I touch your hand again? I'm desperate."

When Bobby has finished seducing Jane in the sordid shambles of the bedroom, he says, "I want my Marianne back." His throat seizes. Tears stream onto his wino face.

"You make me feel like a stand-in."

"You are a stand-in."

This flings Jane into all the ugliness of her trade, and before she can stop herself she says, "I'm going to have your ass evicted if it's the last thing I do. I'll see you in hell."

But then Bobby begins to cry a little, and once again she hates herself for being mean, a sensation Bobby has not experienced. He whimpers, "Please help me." He's beginning to acquire the tiniest bit of a new erection.

During the long day in bed, Bobby tells Jane everything he knows about Marianne, Donna, and Chino. Plus what he heard about Jan and La Costa. He keeps checking to be sure that Jane really knows the town. Too, he likes her hard flat-sided buttocks, her irrational exclamations, and her lingerie. Sometimes he cries a little, but Jane is drawn to him because he is crying less and less. Finally, he has a shower and puts on his striking clothes. How handsome! she will recall thinking.

Chino is in the luxurious living room of his condominium. He is speaking to Max, a hearty mid-forties salmon canner and developer from up north. Chino plays a marvelous new role; compared to the love birds in Presidio Heights, Chino and Max are just plain happier.

"North Beach had grown tiresome, even to me," Chino explains. "The fire escapes made everything a little vulgar. Would you not say so?"

"I accept your work, Donald." Max smiles. Chino has gone back to "Donald Arthur Jones." Max is the only one with manners enough to accept it. The girls keep calling him Chino, as if he were some beaner from down yonder.

"And that one little door with no place to go. And the aging beatniks! Ugh! But that one little door made it seem so much like a drive-up window. I'm no McDonald's!"

"How much is that fresh face?"

"Five hundred dollars."

"Rather steep, isn't it?"

"You know the law. Think of my risk. She's very pretty, very educated. She has no reason to be here."

Max pays him, remarking, "Don't overbook her. A thing like that can lose its bloom overnight."

Chino looks like a pixie as he opens the door to Marianne's room. She lies curled up on an enormous bed covered by a huge, wholesome, handmade quilt. She faces the wall. She hears the door close, then Max's gruff voice: "Get up."

Three in the morning and the same bed. Marianne is bound, gagged, and naked, eerily delineated by a small amount of light that is sufficient, nonetheless, to reveal her tangled hair, stained face, and sense of all-consuming defeat and pollution. The light snaps on and La Costa stands in the doorway staring expressionlessly at Marianne. La Costa's large eyes blink regularly until she has taken it all in. Then she goes into sudden motion, freeing Marianne from the knots that bind her face, hands, and feet. Marianne gets up. The new freedom nauseates her for a moment.

"Are you going to be all right?"

"Yes. Are you La Costa?"

"Uh huh. Why don't you come here and lie down?" La Costa makes the ravaged bed with deft, efficient movements. The elephantine Max twisted everything in his ardor.

"I want some water. I want to walk."

La Costa leads Marianne toward the kitchen, slowly and by the arm.

"When I feel like a child, I cry and suck my thumb. Even in front of a john. But never in front of a pimp. The good pimp has only one weakness, which is his desire to kill whores. He is watching and he is waiting."

"Like a hawk," says Marianne.

Back in Marianne's room you can just make out the two faces as they talk like children at a slumber party.

Marianne asks, "What about Chino, though?"

"I think he's hilarious."

"Hilarious."

"He read that more Americans can recognize the McDonald's hamburger commercial than the national anthem. So he decided he and McDonald's were in direct competition." La Costa begins to sing, "You deserve a break today at McDonald's." But she is interrupted, at first by Marianne's rhythmic sobbing and finally, "I've been raped I've been raped I've been raped." La Costa rests a hand on Marianne's back and looks out the window, slowly shaking her head.

In front of Melvin Belli's office, which is a bogus old San Francisco–style place with a theater-set law library in the front window, two whores are using the reflection to improve their makeup. Belli's occasional appearances on the other side of the glass are of the same order.

About a block away, Bobby gives Jane a send-off. She is dressed pretty much like the girls at the window. They watch her approach warily.

"What's happening?" asks Jane.

"We're innocent, officer," says the first girl, a Chinese.

"I'm looking for a girl I used to know in the life. Name of Donna."

"Madonna?"

"Donna."

"Donna who?"

"Donna from Hamtramck with a chipped tooth."

"Where did you work?" the Chinese girl wants to know.

"Out of a high rise on Sansome. I had a book."

"What'd you quit for?" asks the white girl.

"I didn't like the humiliation." Jane doesn't have her heart in this. She doesn't want to find Donna and she doesn't want to find Marianne. She feels like a dope in this hooker suit Bobby got her. The cheapie sequined pantyhose are squeezing her ass like an anaconda.

The white girl says, "It isn't no humiliation unless you don't get paid. You were never in the life."

"What's the difference? I'm not going to stand here and argue all night. Just tell me where a person could bump into Donna."

"Last time we seen her, which was tonight"—the Chinese girl walks off in disgust and casts a satirical wave to Bobby— "she was working the fake ship at Bernstein's Fish Grotto."

Bobby and Jane glide down Powell Street in a taxi, headed for Bernstein's. The imitation ship's bow projects over the sidewalk. And in front of a window full of back-lit swimming fish stands Donna. The street is Atlantis.

"There she is!"

Bobby jumps out and Donna is gone like a deer. He sprints a few yards and quits. Bobby climbs back in and slumps in real depression.

The driver says, "Give her ten minutes and she'll be in Moar's cafeteria."

At Moar's, Bobby and Jane get out and rush inside. The door nearly slams in Jane's face. Inside, Donna sits beneath Benjamino Bufano murals that depict brotherly love. She's drinking a cup of coffee. They go to her table.

Donna says, "A working girl can't get nowhere today. You've got your nerve."

"I'm Jane Adams."

"Are you with the law?"

"Let's just say I'm helping Bobby find his—find somebody."

"Bobby's a God damned deviate, and he had her up there working for free."

"Up where?"

"Look, I'm not telling anything."

"Would it take money?" Bobby asks.

"No."

"Something. What?"

"Pain pills. Fifty thousand Percodans."

"We could land you in jail."

"So land me."

"Donna," Jane asks, "what's the problem?"

"The problem is I still think my ship will come in. So far, the only one's been at Bernstein's. My cousin married a hippie trial lawyer and got out of the life. They adopted a three-year-old Chicano right off of a Hallmark card and live in Pacific Heights two blocks from the Russian Embassy. What's wrong with that? My only trip to Pacific Heights and I drew a seventy-year-old eye-ear-nose-throat guy and he had a dead monkey in a footlocker. I gave him his money back. You know what? I can't stand it. And I won't talk. And if you don't get out of here, I'm going to start screaming!"

Somehow the next day, by the time La Costa has gotten Marianne to the cable-car stop, Marianne's vitality has begun to return. Pragmatic La Costa is not interested in how Marianne got herself into this; to La Costa, Marianne is another prostitute, and, for instance, we all have a story. She says to Marianne, "I think it's time the rotten little kids had a spree. Marianne, let's go downtown."

They descend Powell Street gazing upon the beautiful

city. When they pass the Bank of America La Costa says, "Many pimps in there."

They head for Gump's department store and proceed to its imperial interior, crossing the great showrooms and on to the Kimono Room, where they play at being old-time courtesans amid the exorbitant women's clothing. La Costa fills their purses with silk scarves. When Marianne looks startled, La Costa says, "If we're nabbed, yell 'racist.' Tell them you're high yellow."

On this same day, Bobby and Jane are downtown shopping in a glamorous Maiden Lane pet store, a splendid room full of South American birds, very carefully observed by an ocelot with an aqua collar.

Bobby explains everything. "I can't have another day without a hawk. And the only thing legal here is a Colombian broadwing, which is not a first-class hawk."

"I don't know one from another," Jane says, shyly gazing at Bobby.

When the shrouded cage rests on the back seat of the cab between Bobby and Jane, she says demurely, "I always thought hawks just killed chickens."

Bobby sighs. "That's only part of the story, Jane."

Inside the Presidio Heights house, Bobby sets the cage on the floor and removes the shroud.

"Open the cage, Jane."

"I'm afraid."

"Open the cage."

Jane gingerly opens the cage and the hawk comes out, flying around the room with terrible beating wings, to settle finally on the back of the tall chair, where it stares with un-forgiving yellow eyes at the amateur pimp and his realtor friend.

□ □ □

The middle of the night at Quickee Char-Broil can be lonesome. The chef sweeps the little flaming pieces of meat onto a tray with salad and hands them over to Chino and Donna. Then the cook becomes the cashier and takes Donna's money. Condominium Donald is Cheapo Chino again.

Donna carries the tray to the table and puts the meals down carefully. She aches with love. The two sit. Immediately, Chino swaps plates.

"I said rare." He fills his mouth. "That other God damn thing's like a baseball glove. How'd you do?"

"Four hundred."

"Give it ta me."

Donna hands him the money proudly. Now is her opportunity.

"I want to work in the condo."

"No room."

"I'm tired."

"You want to go back to Petaluma?"

"I'm not from Petaluma."

"I know a big-time Jap chicken farmer. I'll send your ass to him in Petaluma."

"I brought you Marianne, and now I'm working the hotels and she's in the condo. That's not fair."

What an outburst. Chino reaches and seizes her steak in his hand. He squeezes it until beef blood runs between his fingers.

"You shit too," he says. "See that? That's your Petaluma face. Gimme your napkin."

Chino puts her steak down and wipes his hands. He continues, upon reflection.

"Don't give me no eye. Looking at me like you got nothing to eat." Impulsively, he shoves the steak down her blouse. Tears stream as the steak bleeds through. Chino is on the verge of raving. " 'I wanna be in the condo, I wanna be in the condo.' How much room you think is there? Huh? Look, I'm no McDonald's." He stands in total disgust and turns to the staring fry cook. "Hey." He menaces him. "Try going blind." He turns back to Donna, his original fury intact. "I'll give you a condo. Petaluma Jap chicken condo. I give up."

He upends her purse on the table.

"What are you doing?"

"I'm gonna make sure there isn't something in here I should know about. What's this?"

"Herbal Essence Shampoo."

"What about this crap?"

"It's for dry-skin relief. It's by Revlon."

"This is the biggest bottle of Excedrin I've ever seen. What's this?"

"Silverfrost. It's an eye shadow. Also by Revlon. That little box? That's Aziza two-tone luster shadow."

"What about this?"

"Supernails."

Chino pulls out an eyelash curler and tries it on himself. Donna is crying, but she thinks he's cute. Then a green jar. His face is a question mark.

Donna says, "That's analgesic balm, for small injuries."

"Let me ask you something, Miss Whore. Why don't you take your repair kit and get the fuck out of my life?"

"I don't want to."

"Then bring me Marianne's boyfriend. Get him drunk first. Otherwise you're too ugly to get the job done."

The condo in the gloaming: long blades of bayside light penetrate the cloud-high dwelling. Marianne is in her room with her new friend, who, dressed for the street, turns shining African eyes on getting it while she can. Marianne is dressed in silk pajamas, part of the basic issue, suggesting a youthful housewife caught in an unsavory trap. Thanks to La Costa, she's confident she can do a walk-through, keeping her mind's eye on a better day. Meanwhile, she's trying to explain Bobby. She says he must have caught her at the right time. She thinks maybe she fell in love with him or, as so many young women say, "I thought so at the time." "Sometimes," says Marianne, "you find yourself counting how long you've been away from home and sometimes you know you'll never get there again."

The door bangs open: Chino.

"You want to head out, La Costa? Marianne's got a visitor." La Costa makes a little comic rotary wave and leaves. Then Chino leaves, somewhat in La Costa's wake, and the door is closed like the shutter of a stalled-out camera. When it blinks open again a huge wavering figure appears and closes the door. This is an enormous man. His tiny briefs are lost in the declivity of flesh that is the last fold of his belly. He's about fifty and has the ponderous face of an oaf and the baleful gazing eyes we associate with martyrs whose stories have been lost.

"Do you like me?" he wants to know. His ring finger hooks the corner of his minute briefs. Desperately, Marianne recalls the buffalo paddock, the fog, the lost, adventurous dreaming of long ago. It was coming at her.

Chino and La Costa are watching a Western on TV.

Chino says, "Guy in there with Marianne?"

"Yeah?"

"He designs golf courses."

"Is that so."

"His wife's a concert pianist, but he made her quit."

"What's he gonna make Marianne do?"

"No telling."

La Costa is staring at the television. "Is that Montgomery Clift?"

"I don't know."

"I think he's about to kick John Wayne's butt. Don't he just move his eyes cute, though?"

The golf-course designer appears in a blue suit.

"Highly overrated," he says.

Chino stares, at a loss for words.

"And this pitch about resistance? I'm glad it's on your phone bill. I'll tell you what she is: she's a whore. I saw through her in a minute. She's simply a prostitute like Mandy there. Don't call me again. I can do better at the Masters in Augusta."

Chino is abashed. This topflight professional has made him feel like a crumbum. Then he's mad. He's infected with anger. It's like some incoherent mind scabies crying for a final scratch. He makes no remark as the golf-course designer shoves open the door and leaves.

Dusty and battered after a long fight, Montgomery Clift and John Wayne are casting glances of new-won respect at each other. There's a big free sky behind them as well as admiring townspeople to watch them become friends.

Chino stares at the screen, trying to get his bearings.

In the kitchen in Presidio Heights, Jane, pressing out little silhouette men on a buttered cookie sheet, has to dust her hands to answer the door. It is Donna, and she tells Jane how to find Marianne.

La Costa makes up Marianne's eyes and powders her golden cheeks with a sable brush. Neither of them says a word.

Bobby comes in from the Palace of the Legion of Honor, where he saw a documentary about the end of the elephants. "They had these fabulous aerial photographs of elephants in their death throes. Then there was this terrific shot of an enormous bull who had died long ago, and all he was was like this terrible emblem on the desert floor."

Jane replies, "You can find Marianne any night after nine in the Room of the Dons at the Mark Hopkins. She's a whore." Then Jane says to Bobby, "Stay with me."

Bobby says, "Stay with you? Without your cross-referenced street guide, I wouldn't have been with you in the first place."

The Room of the Dons is a dark, paneled room. Marianne sits at the bar against the backdrop of paintings that depict the mythical Amazons of an imaginary California. Bobby sits next to her and rests his head on her shoulder. He holds her arm in both of his hands.

"Oh, my baby."

"Hello, Bobby."

"Has it been awful?"

"No."

"Can we go?"

"We need a room."

"Can we go home?" says Bobby.

"I've got a place."

Once they're inside Marianne's room in the condominum, Bobby turns his eyes toward her in terrified suspension. He walks to the window and its pricey vista.

"Am I going to have to pay?" he asks.

"Yes."

"Then I think you're trapped."

"No, you are," she says.

Bobby hands her his wallet. "I don't want to hear the numbers. Take out how much it is."

Marianne peels the bills into her purse and gives Bobby his wallet back.

"Shall I undress you?" she asks.

"Did you take out for that?"

"I took out for everything," she says slowly. And for once in Bobby's life pure desire pours through him like flame. For once.

Having quietly let himself in, Chino waits his turn in the front room. But, as with Bobby, nothing happens quite as he has foreseen it. Because Marianne's door bursts open and Bobby flings himself into the hallway, a knife plunged in the base of his neck, jetting fatal quantities of blood on everything. Bobby clambers down the hallway toward Chino like a bride in a dream, smearing the walls as he goes, reaching, reaching toward the only man in the place.

The bloody bed is repeatedly ignited by flashbulbs. The officer turns to the press for a moment of candor. The people have to know. A stretcher passes covered with a sheet, the anonymous contents of which constitute a valediction to every long walk off every short pier in America.

The officer says, "We have no clues. Okay? You can see he was well off. He has no record of employment. Y'with me so far? Perhaps he was living on a trust fund. Since we don't know what was here, we don't know what was stolen. I think there's a very real chance that, as a man of independent means, he kept too many valuables around. Okay? Such men are very relaxed about their possessions. You could pick the lock; you could buy the doorman. There's more than one way to skin a cat. But this much is certain: I cannot offer any encouragement that your readers will ever hear the end of this story."

Thomas McGuane is the author of several highly acclaimed novels, including *Nothing But Blue Skies; Keep the Change; The Sporting Club; The Bushwhacked Piano,* which won the Richard and Hilda Rosenthal Award of the American Academy and Institute of Arts and Letters; *Ninety-Two in the Shade,* which was nominated for the National Book Award; *Panama; Nobody's Angel; Something to Be Desired;* and *An Outside Chance,* a collection of essays on sport.

Thomas McGuane lives in Montana.

Also available from Vintage Contemporaries

Picturing Will
by Ann Beattie

An absorbing novel of a curious five-year-old and the adults who surround him.

"Beattie's best novel since *Chilly Scenes of Winter* ... its depth and movement are a revelation." —*The New York Times Book Review*

0-679-73194-6/$9.95

Where I'm Calling From
by Raymond Carver

The summation of a triumphant career from "one of the great short story writers of our time—of any time" *(Philadelphia Inquirer)*.

0-679-72231-9/$11.00

The House on Mango Street
by Sandra Cisneros

Told in a series of vignettes stunning for their eloquence, the story of a young girl growing up in the Hispanic quarter of Chicago.

"Cisneros is one of the most brilliant of today's young writers. Her work is sensitive, alert, nuanceful ... rich with music and picture." —Gwendolyn Brooks

0-679-73477-5/$9.00

Wildlife
by Richard Ford

Set in Great Falls, Montana, an absorbing novel of a family tested to the breaking point.

"Ford brings the early Hemingway to mind. Not many writers can survive the comparison. Ford can. *Wildlife* has a look of permanence about it." —*Newsweek*

0-679-73447-3/$9.00

The Chosen Place, the Timeless People
by Paule Marshall

A novel set on a devastated part of a Caribbean island, whose tense relationships—between natives and foreigners, blacks and whites, haves and have-nots—keenly dramatize the vicissitudes of power.

"Unforgettable ... monumental." —*Washington Post Book World*

0-394-72633-2/$13.00

Bright Lights, Big City
by Jay McInerney

Living in Manhattan as if he owned it, a young man tries to outstrip the approach of dawn with nothing but his wit, good will and controlled substances in this celebrated novel.

"A dazzling debut, smart, hearfelt, and very, very funny."   —Tobias Wolff

0-394-72641-3/$9.00

Mama Day
by Gloria Naylor

This magical tale of a Georgia sea island centers around a powerful and loving matriarch who can call up lightning storms and see secrets in her dreams.

"This is a wonderful novel, full of spirit and sass and wisdom."   —*Washington Post*

0-679-72181-9/$10.00

Anywhere But Here
by Mona Simpson

An extraordinary novel that is at once a portrait of a mother and daughter and a brilliant exploration of the perennial urge to keep moving.

"Mona Simpson takes on—and reinvents—many of America's essential myths ... stunning."   —*The New York Times*

0-679-73738-3/$11.00

The Joy Luck Club
by Amy Tan

"Vivid ... wondrous ... what it is to be American, and a woman, mother, daughter, lover, wife, sister and friend—these are the troubling, loving alliances and affiliations that Tan molds into this remarkable novel."   —*San Francisco Chronicle*

"A jewel of a book."   —*The New York Times Book Review*

0-679-72768-X/$10.00

Philadelphia Fire
by John Edgar Wideman

"Reminiscent of Ralph Ellison's *Invisible Man*" *(Time)*, this powerful novel is based on the 1985 bombing by police of a West Philadelphia row house owned by the Afro-centric cult, Move.

"A book brimming over with brutal, emotional honesty and moments of beautiful prose lyricism."   —Charles Johnson, *Washington Post Book World*

0-679-73650-6/$10.00

• •

Available at your local bookstore,
or call toll-free to order: 1-800-733-3000
(credit cards only). Prices subject to change.

**VINTAGE
CONTEMPORARIES**